W9-BKY-809

PRAISE FOR *UNTRACEABLE*

"Enthralling and exquisite, by one of modern Russia's finest writers."
—PHILIPPE SANDS,
author of *East West Street: On the Origins of*
"Genocide" and "Crimes against Humanity"

"The darkest impulses of science and power cross paths with human error and plots gone awry in Sergei Lebedev's incisive and all-too-plausible Russian novel about nerve agents, assassination and secrets both political and personal."
—WILL ENGLUND,
Pulitzer Prize-winning former Moscow correspondent for
The Washington Post and author of
March 1917: On the Brink of War and Revolution

"Sergei Lebedev is a marvelous writer with two rare gifts: a nobility of style and the most precise inner vision, which allows him to see and plumb the entire depth of the anthropological catastrophe that occurred in twentieth-century Russia. Lebedev has perceived what was invisible to most Soviet and post-Soviet writers."
—VLADIMIR SOROKIN,
author of *The Blizzard, Day of the Oprichnik* and *Ice Trilogy*

UNTRACEABLE

A NOVEL

SERGEI LEBEDEV

TRANSLATED FROM THE RUSSIAN BY ANTONINA W. BOUIS

NEW VESSEL PRESS
NEW YORK

New Vessel Press

www.newvesselpress.com

First published in Russian in 2020 as *Debutant*

Copyright © 2019 Sergei Lebedev
Translation Copyright © 2021 Antonina W. Bouis

Library of Congress Cataloging-in-Publication Data
Lebedev, Sergei
[Debutant, English]
Untraceable/Sergei Lebedev; translation by Antonina W. Bouis.
p. cm.

ISBN 978-1-939931-90-0
Library of Congress Control Number 2020935328
I. Russia—Fiction

Homunculus (From the phial, to Wagner.)
Now, father! That was no joke. How are you?
Come: press me tenderly to your heart, too!
But not too hard, the glass may be too thin.
It's in the very nature of the thing:
For the natural the world has barely space:
What's artificial commands a narrow place.
(To Mephistopheles.)
But you, Rascal, my dear Cousin, are you
Here at the right moment? I thank you, too.
Good fortune's led you here to me:
Since I exist, I must be doing, you see.
I'd like to begin my work today:
You're skillful at shortening the way.

Faust Part 2, Goethe

CHAPTER 1

Vyrin had grown accustomed to the muted, prolonged ailments that accompanied the approach of old age. But he felt the aches and pains more acutely in summer than in any other season. They ripened and gathered strength by late August, the anniversary of his defection, tormenting his joints, vessels, and eyeballs—only to vanish with ease in early fall, when the heat abated and the barometer calmed down.

Maybe this was the death sentence given me in absentia, he joked to himself, his lips tasting the wormwood of death postponed.

"Or is my body taking its revenge?" he thought. "Revenge for the new face created by the plastic surgeon? The scars and birthmarks lasered away? Does it remember and prepare its revenge on the anniversary of my defection?"

He had persistent conjunctivitis from the contact lenses that altered his eye color. His legs ached from the lifts in his shoes. His hair was brittle from the dye. Being someone else entailed intensive daily labor. He couldn't get used to it.

Formally, the previous person no longer existed. There was another one now. A foundling, a changeling, with a biography created by masters of lies and transformations.

A different language. Different habits. Even his dreams were different. A different memory that seemed to have subsumed the old one.

The new identity fit him like a prosthetic device; seldom did it feel like a natural part of him.

His body, redrawn by a scalpel, remembered—the visceral memory of guts, liver, and kidneys, where the by-products of existence settle and crystalize, like gallstones and kidney stones. It resisted, even though there was no returning to the past for Vyrin; the banal and metaphorical sentence had a direct juridical force as well.

He learned not to suppress but to value and observe sym-pathetically the stubbornness of aging flesh, denying the fake, imposed sacrament of second birth. Body, you are the only thing I have left, he would sometimes say with a strange adolescent tenderness. His body truly was the only material evidence that he had once been someone else.

There was other evidence, which he could not access or con-trol. A paper ghost. A spare duplicate of his life. An archival *I* that ordinary people did not possess.

An officer's personnel file.

The extract and essence of his previous self. Not yet a defec-tor. Not yet a traitor.

A light-blue cardboard file. 225 x 330 x 25 mm. Even those dimensions are secret.

Photo ID. File. Autobiography. Employment report. Non-disclosure agreement. Special profiling. Endurance test: three-kilometer cross-country run. Character assessments: documents, documents, documents.

He knew that after his defection an order was promulgated, labeled Top Secret with two zeroes as the number of the case document and headed: "On Measures in Connection with A. V. Vyrin's Treason." He had heard such orders read out in the Secretariat—about other men. All the same, as if written on carbon paper. "Ideological transformation. Moral collapse. Take measures to localize the consequences of treason." Only the names of the people to be punished were changed: personnel officers, heads of education departments, heads of subdepartments who had not shown adequate diligence and had not recognized a potential traitor in time.

But he knew that in his case the public reprimands were for naught. He had served the system with more loyalty than the others. And he was more frightened than the others when the country began falling apart and it looked as if the system would collapse with it.

Vyrin told himself that almost three decades had now passed and the information he had revealed, the agents he had disclosed, were no longer important. The agents would have been burned anyway; someone else would have given them away if not I. I managed to sell them in time, like currency that would soon drop in value catastrophically; another year or two and who would need, say, information on agents among anti-Soviet émigrés or in the ranks of European communist parties? If the USSR itself no longer existed?

Reasoning rationally, Vyrin thought he was relatively safe. But back beyond the border of his homeland, which he could not cross, his personnel file was like a voodoo doll into which the priest could stick his deadly needles at any moment.

That is why he occasionally felt unexplained anxiety, examining arms, belly, neck, and face for unusual rashes, papillomas, those strange signs that prophetic nature sometimes sends people. During those moments he felt there was a vague, fatal connection between flesh and paper; that the document remaining in the archives could sense and therefore knew more than what was written on it, that it had a one-dimensional soul of a fury that could only seek and avenge.

Paper wants blood, he would whisper as he recalled how he was given heavy cardboard files: notes on operational surveillance, notes on operational resolution. Back then he was the beater who drove the prey, not the wild game being hunted. He dealt with people who were exiled, fled, or moved to the West. They left, but their files remained in the archives; if necessary, the files were retrieved or raised—they had this expression in the service, "raising out of the archives."

Out of the cellar. Out of the depths. From the bottom.

The case files had everything. Thousands of pages. Transcripts of telephone conversations. Agent communications. Surveillance reports. "In the morning the subject did not leave the house and was not visited by persons known to intelligence. At 16:05 a car drove into the building courtyard . . . " "At 10:05 the subject left the building for the bakery, where he bought a loaf of white bread."

The pale letters—the typewriter ribbon was worn—seemed to reflect the weakness and anemia of those under surveillance. He remembered thousands of such lines. Their ordinariness used to serve as an aphrodisiac; a visual embodiment of the power of their agency and the insignificance of its domestic enemies—bugs, insects under a loupe.

Now with a new life in a free country, he thought that what he had been reading was a novel by a paranoid author, a text of texts written by a mad state machine of memory. A novel that pursued the extreme aim of capturing life in its entirety and creating a copy for the police.

The state, however, is always a Cyclops; its gaze is not stereoscopic, it is one-sided. It sees only murky signs of loyalty and disloyalty. Reflections of prior suspicions that take illusory form in random events. Therefore a dossier, he thought, is not a duplicate of life. It is a special, dark, truncated twin, fabricated from denunciations, stolen, eavesdropped words, covertly observed scenes; the source of the secret, evil power comprising the ability to tear off the protective covers of quotidian life.

He had created such twins, to use them in the hunt for people.

Now they were hunting him.

Vyrin could not prove that. He could only detect it, feel it with the victim's sixth sense. He knew nothing for sure, their service did not share its secrets, even within itself. He merely guessed that there was—could have been—one more unspoken order, the shadow of that headed: "On Measures in Connection with Treason . . ." The order was also a sentence. Back in the 1990s, Vyrin had given evidence to the police, who were investigating the commercial ties of his former colleagues with fake businesses transferring and laundering money. Back then it seemed harmless. Now it did not.

Psychologists had warned him that he might experience an irrational urge to go to the embassy and turn himself in. Or that he would take ridiculous risks, stupidly overlook the rules of conspiracy, subconsciously try to be exposed.

He had never felt anything like that.

But he did not tell the psychologists that he had a superstitious fear of something quite different: a bad coincidence, some insignificant stray incident, a fatal trifle, an absurdity. Like what happened last month: Vyrin received an official notification in the mail that he had been selected for jury duty.

A lottery, a random hit: a computer program selected him out of the three hundred thousand residents of the city. You could even say it was a good sign, confirmation that his faked identity did not arouse any suspicions among the uninformed bureaucrats and that he was treated like everyone else.

But he tensed up. As if he felt an evil gaze, foreign, seeking contact. They had promised him from the start that his new name would not appear in official registries or on lists. He had to call the officer handling him, who apologized and promised they would get rid of his name; allegedly, the court system had upgraded its program and compatible databases, and that's how the error occurred.

Vyrin insisted that they use the ordinary, legal way and get an excuse for health reasons. That way there would be no electronic trace that could even obliquely indicate Mr. Mihalski's special status. The officer merely chuckled politely.

His former handler still remembered the Cold War. The Wall. He had recently retired. The new guy was just over thirty. When Vyrin defected, the officer was in kindergarten. He probably considered Vyrin superfluous detritus, an old man's junk forgotten in the attic.

He must think the boredom is getting to me, Vyrin thought.

His immediate response was to leave. But he changed his

mind right away: if they were watching him, a hasty departure could give him away. So Vyrin lived a month adhering strictly, even excessively, to his routine behavior as an unsociable bachelor pensioner.

The gnawing anxiety passed; only the usual and tiresome ailments remained.

August had just begun. In the mornings, the farmers' market was filled with the golden buzz of wasps hovering over glistening mounds of burgundy cherries, used in a famous local cake.

The cherries were slightly fermented. In all his travels he had never seen fruit like this, Goliaths among cherries, so large they were disproportionate, ungainly giants. Vyrin bought some seemingly flawless sweet cherries, but could not eat the whole bag: there was too little flavor, dead fruit flesh; it was like kissing unresponsive lips in a narcotic sleep.

He decided to take his favorite long walk, a reward for the many weeks indoors. Starting at the river that divided the city in two, full and murky after the rains; its crazed waters, flying, turning to foam, then becoming a wave; repeatedly changing its nature every second. Vyrin went into the hills, the forest, dark even on a sunny summer day.

He went up the street that led away from the main square, past a house beloved by sightseers with a dormer roof projecting over the street and under which stood an outlandish statue: a mustached Janissary in a painted vest, scimitar in his right hand, shield in his left; it was a reminder of the ruthless Turkish siege, the former threat from the East.

Vyrin no longer looked at the city as a tourist. He was not amused by the dancing figures in the church clock, or the steep funicular, or the tunnels through the castle mountain. However, this lone assassin with two moons on his shield, crescents turned away from each other, like reverse parentheses—a divinity of a dangerous moment, an evil hour—was not a mere amusement for Vyrin. He felt that if a killer were to come for his soul, the Janissary would warn him, give him a sign.

Tourists crowded around the house with the Janissary. He heard the words of his native tongue spoken fluently—after his isolation they sounded so unexpected and piercing, as if they contained a hidden meaning unknown to the speaker himself. Vyrin smoothly crossed the street and looked, without turning his head, at the reflection in a store window: nothing special, a Sunday excursion.

Blocks of individual houses. The botanical gardens on the outskirts. The windows of the greenhouses were fogged from inside, as if the alien tropical vegetation had adopted the predatory ways of reptiles and insects and was exhaling hotly, oozing toxic sweat, gathering strength to escape outside.

Vyrin reached the dirt road, zigzagging up the valley slopes.

The forest was fabulously immense. It grew along the swollen slopes of the limestone ridge, falling steeply into the misty undergrowth, the green loam of ferns and mosses. Distances were lost in it, and the road looped sharply, with the sun shining sometimes from the right, then from the left. Just when you thought that you had lost your way, the cathedral bell rang out rich and clear in the distance; actually, it was the resonant response of the bell's brass—edifying, encouraging, and dissipating all anxiety—that Vyrin liked about this path through old firs, reminiscent of the forests of his childhood.

He walked, feeling his body fill with blessed tiredness. Vyrin knew every root, every hole on this path, and he looked forward to seeing the pasture on the left, fenced by rowan trees—the berries would be ripe in color by now—and then he would encounter the sweet, gentle chimney smoke from the farm. The walk both tired and invigorated him; his recent fears seemed silly. I guess I really am old, he thought. I've become neurotically fearful.

He could see the cathedral from the last turn. It stood on a stone outcropping that divided the top of the valley. The yellow façade, framed by two bell towers, continued upward from the vertical plane of the cliff. This church was much larger than the cathedral in town. It had been built here, in the mountains, by the pass, on an ancient pilgrimage path, its majestic vaults signifying the depth and significance of someone's epiphany, an acquisition of faith that took place in the silent solitude of the outcropping.

Beyond the cathedral's back wall, in the shade of chestnut trees, lay a small outdoor restaurant with good food. The regular waiters recognized him—or pretended to. They did not try to chat but smiled respectfully. Here he fully felt he was Mr. Mihalski; he took that pleasant and exciting sense of connection, the merging of true and invented identities, as a special gift which he brought back home in the trolley that traveled along the bottom of the valley.

Today the courtyard was full: a summer weekend. There was only one free table, at the edge behind a wide-branching tree. Next to the sandbox and swings. That meant frenzied children would run around, making noise. Vyrin preferred sitting among people dining sedately, behind strangers, in the buzz of calm conversation, the clinking of knives and forks, where it is hard to eavesdrop, photograph, or take aim.

Vyrin looked at the diners: Was anyone about to leave? No, they were all relaxed, in a merry lazy mood. The brunette at the nearby table had a provocative drop of crème brûlée on her upper lip. She didn't wipe it away or lick it off, knowing how seductive and sexy it looked. She wore a dark metal necklace resembling a dog collar—a sign of exotic passions, kinky torment insolently displayed in a restaurant by a church.

The brunette's sister, in her eighth month at least—her swollen belly had pulled her dress up to reveal strong, plump legs—was eating chocolate cake and schnitzel simultaneously with great appetite, as if the infant were overripe, born but remaining in the womb, and demanding his share of the feast.

Vyrin wanted to leave. He was dizzy with fatigue, the heavy scents, the density of human voices—the village was small, everyone was related in some cousinhood, redolent of fetid incest that repulses outsiders like salty seawater.

But he felt the charm of the play of light in the chestnut leaves, the clay-blue tablecloths pressed so that there wasn't a single wrinkle, the high-necked bottles of ice water, the harmless murmur of neighbors, the balletic moves of waiters balancing enormous trays of six to eight plates on their shoulders, where atop the delicately tossed salad looking as if arranged by a coiffeur, the leaves green with reddish veins, floated golden-breaded schnitzels, resembling torn blobs of copper blasted from a smelting furnace.

Yum, yum, yum the pregnant woman crooned to her unborn infant. The limestone angel with a blurred face blew silently into a golden trumpet over the back entrance to the church. He felt himself basking in the insouciant summer that enveloped the entire world.

Vyrin ordered beer and a steak. Wasps flew toward the fragrant hops. They were not attracted by the remains of dessert on nearby plates, rivulets of honey and chocolate—only by hops. They crawled around the rim of the mug and tried to land on his shoulder, his hand, circling persistently and stubbornly. He waved them away, almost spilling his beer. He had a bad allergy to insect bites. Back when he was in the service, the doctors said it would get worse over the years and offered to give him a medical discharge. Wasps, wasps, wasps—he moved the mug away, flicked a wasp, and then another, from the table, regretting he had not brought a jacket.

A sting. On the nape of his bare neck. Sudden. As painful as an injection administered by an inexperienced nurse.

He slapped the bite, but the wasp was gone. He turned, intent on the pain, and noticed a man walking away and getting into a car. The license plates were not local.

His neck ached. The pain spread up and down, to his shoulder, cheek, temple. He felt something microscopic in the wound—probably the stinger.

His vision clouded. His breathing became shallow. His body was engulfed by dry heat. He got up with difficulty and headed for the toilet.

Rinse. He needed to rinse with cold water. Take a pill. But wash first. Such pressure in his throat! He might not be able to swallow the pill. His skin was burning.

He could barely stand. He leaned against the sink, clumsily splashed water on his face. The wasp sting was on the right side of his neck, and his right arm was stiff. He shoved the tablet into his throat. The mirror showed a gray, bloodless, but swollen face, as if something was trying to undo the plastic surgery and force his old look back on him.

The tablet should have worked by now. It was the latest medicine.

But it wasn't working.

A rash broke out on the gray skin. His stomach cramped. He sank to the floor, staring at the tiles—and understood. That man had not been a customer at the restaurant. Locals didn't park where he had stopped the car.

With a final effort, he rose and holding on to the walls made his way into the corridor. His constricted throat kept him from screaming, calling for help. On the porch, he bumped into a waiter carrying a tray of bottles and wineglasses. The waiter assumed he was dead drunk and moved aside. He fell from the porch, taking the waiter with him, hearing the crashing glass and hoping that everyone noticed and was looking. He hissed and gurgled into someone's ear:

"Ambulance...police...murder...not drunk...poison... I was poisoned."

And he collapsed, still hearing the sounds of the world but no longer understanding what they meant.

CHAPTER 2

The two generals had known each other a long time. They had served together under the red flag with hammer and sickle.

The lieutenant general had been chairman of the Party Committee then. And secretly, he was head of the numbered department, which was not indicated even in the top-secret staff register. The major general had been his deputy, successor, rival. The Party Committee was long since disbanded. But the department remained. It survived all the reforms of their agency, all the changes in names and leaders, divisions and mergers. As ever, it had only a number and was not included on the organizational chart.

They were in the surveillance-free room and could talk without worry of being overheard. However, their language, laden with professional euphemisms, deceitful by nature, allowed the men to formulate sentences so that they could be interpreted as expressing either conviction or doubt.

They both knew that their conversation would most likely result in the execution of an order, unspoken, not registered in the system of secret case files, but which would still require sanction at the very top. Both generals wanted to avoid responsibility for a possible failure but to claim his share of benefits in case of success. Each knew what the other was thinking.

"According to the information of our neighbors, he died after four days in an induced coma. The organism almost coped with it, you might say. We can't rule out that the dose was insufficient. Or its method of introduction was wrong. Perhaps he had time to take antidote pills. Or some other outside substance lowered the effectiveness of the preparation. Weather could have been a factor. Air pressure. It was in the mountains, high altitude. Before passing out, he had time to say he had been attacked. The waiter was a former policeman. Someone else might not have paid attention, thought it was just a drunken fantasy."

"So did the neighbors want the incident to attract attention or not?"

"Naturally, they don't give us details. They may want to put a good face on a bad game: that they had anticipated this becoming public from the start."

"Well then . . . Let's move on to our information."

"An interagency investigation team has been set up. International protocols have been put into action. They're bringing in foreign chemistry experts. There are very few specialists of that quality. They called in four people. Three are known to us, they are on file. They are people with big names. But the fourth one does not appear in the files. There is no open information about him. At our request, competent agents have been questioned. No one has heard of such a scientist. We are continuing the search; we've put the overseas stations on it."

"Looks as if he's a know-nothing, unknown professor."

Both gave a restrained chuckle.

"The source says that this professor was not involved in police cases before. He might have been used by the military, but the source does not know about that. The source is not directly involved in the investigation. His future abilities are limited. He is only coordinating the cooperation of his country's police."

The generals fell silent. They could picture the bureaucratic strategy in an extreme event: controlled chaos, mountains of paperwork, coordination, documents that have to be shared with other agencies. Forced repeal of secrecy regulations. Temporary commissions. Outside specialists who would otherwise never be allowed through the door. Whether the neighbors' action had gone according to plan or not, it gave them a wonderful opportunity, which the neighbors did not recognize.

"There is a high likelihood that this professor is Kalitin," the deputy said at last.

"Yes, that probability exists. It fits his scientific profile. Exactly. And since suspicion naturally falls on our country, it's very reasonable to bring him in. If, of course, he is still alive. And of sound mind."

"He's only seventy. I assume he takes good care of his health. Physical and mental."

"We have an address?"

"The source reported it."

"Will that compromise the source?"

"Can't say with certainty."

"Is he valuable?"

"Moderately. Because of his past in the GDR he has not been promoted readily. And he'll be retiring soon."

"Understood. An order must be given to the station. Let them check it out. Send the very best."

"If they determine it's him, we can prepare the event. And start the coordination."

"Interesting. If it's Kalitin, then it's very interesting."

"Neophyte."

"Yes. Neophyte. His favorite."

"None of our operatives today have worked with Neophyte."

"I am aware of that."

"But there is one candidate—Shershnev. He did an operation with one of Kalitin's early versions. He doesn't have any experience abroad, however. But he was born and grew up there. His father was in our army. He knows the language well. Here's his file."

"I'll take a look. Send all the necessary orders immediately."

"Yes, sir."

The deputy left the room.

The general opened the file.

CHAPTER 3

The bowl and snake. The Bowl of Hygeia.

Kalitin sometimes thought this emblem, inconspicuous and familiar, was persecuting him.

Pharmacy signs. Ubiquitous ambulances. Labels on medicines. Hospital reception areas. Badges on medical personnel. He had almost learned to not be bothered, to pay no attention, not take it personally.

But not right now.

The doctors' suspicions raised his own suspicions, which the doctors must not know. What was happening to his body could be the delayed reaction to long-ago experiments, the surf from yesterday's wave. He had always followed safety measures exactingly, but his substances were too unpredictable, unmanageable to be fully understood. His children. His legacy.

Some of the medical procedures required local anesthesia.

The drug the anesthesiologist used had a hidden and harmless side effect, something like a weak, amateur truth serum. Kalitin experienced vivid and clear—almost digital—memories, sentimental dreams about the past, things he had not thought about for years.

He was a child again, a schoolboy, an obedient son, who had not yet found his calling and his mentor. He was at the stage of development where a child's ability to fill the world with great mysteries and to experience horror and joy in the face of the inexplicable mixed with the beginnings of a rational autobiography; it is in this living contradiction—sometimes, and not in every life—that attractions, desires, symbols, and profound predeterminations of destiny are born.

. . . Every Easter his parents take him to visit Uncle Igor.

Actually, the boy does not know what Easter is. They make blini during the week before Lent. For Easter they dye eggs in onion peel water and bake *kulich* bread. Is that a holiday? It's not listed on the wall calendar. They don't mention it at school. His parents don't seem to know why Easter should be celebrated. They wouldn't do it on their own, he thinks. But if Uncle Igor invites you, you can't say no. He calls on the telephone and names the day; not a word about Easter over the telephone, it is understood.

Who was Uncle Igor? The boy senses that he is not his real uncle. Or, rather, not quite an uncle—there was a blood tie, but it was complicated, requiring a meticulous, apothecary-like examination of units of relatedness, going through the old photo albums, which are kept in a distant corner and cannot be viewed without an adult. There, among the unfamiliar faces, unknown places, landscapes, houses, and idyllic backdrops used by provincial photography studios, a woman will appear in a white dress, sitting at the gigantic anthracite grand piano, looking at the cryptic musical notation. She would be the beginning of a mysterious chain of corporeal transformations from thin to fat, tall to short, dark to blond and back again, with the final link being Uncle Igor.

The boy had already learned that it was better not to ask about some people in the photographs. They wouldn't tell him or they would make up some nonsense. However, it was all right to ask about the people around them, the neighbors, his father's coworkers.

About all of them except Uncle Igor.

They lived in the new City. Ten years earlier it had been unpopulated taiga here. So they are all new settlers, enthusiasts; that's how they are honored in official speeches. The City is surrounded by a Wall: a gray concrete fence with barbed wire. The Wall was built with room to grow: dug-up empty lots lie between it and the residential areas. Because of the Wall, they can't be called on a home phone. Or get mail at home. Or have visitors. Their City does not exist on maps, in reference books, or in atlases. Passenger trains do not go there. Ordinary planes do not fly there. The newspapers don't write about the City. The radio does not mention it. It is not shown on television. It is called Sovetsk-22. For the residents, it is simply the City.

The boy has no memory of being beyond the Wall. But he does know where he and his parents came from—his mother often misses the capital, where his parents were born, where they studied and met, where his grandmothers and aunt live.

Uncle Igor seems to have been born here. Appearing together with the City. Right in the six-room apartment on the third floor of a building that everyone in the City calls the House.

When someone says, "We're moving into the House soon," everyone knows with envy which house they mean. The one on

Revolution Street. The most famous one in the City. Nine stories. With columns at the entrance and molding under the cornices. With handles on the doors that lead into lobbies, where visitors are met by the guard. With high ceilings and enormous apartments. With two elevators in every entry.

The rumors say there were supposed to be several such houses. But for some reason, only one was built. It was a big honor to live there. Father sometimes says that maybe one day they would get an apartment there. Mother turns her head and smiles sadly, ironically.

None of the boy's classmates has ever been in the House. But he has. The House itself is not very interesting. It's only a shell—in fact, molded shells support the cornices of the House—that surrounds the secrets of Uncle Igor's life.

His parents seem to feel it. His father doesn't like it. He would rather not bring him there. A different circle, he says. But Uncle Igor invites all three of them. His otherwise intractable father can't disobey. Why? The boy wants to know.

His mother... Once, when his father was out, the boy secretly watched her trying on a robe, a birthday present from Uncle Igor. Not from here, unearthly, thin burgundy silk, embroidered with birds, flowers, and dragons. She looked in the mirror, pulling it tighter to show her figure then letting the robe's long skirts open freely. May light splashed from the mirror. The yellow lotus leaves trembled. Twisting passionately and hugging her hips, the silver-and-gold dragons with emerald eyes breathed bead and pearl smoke from their broad violet nostrils. Dressed, she was so naked about her feelings that the boy grew embarrassed and shut the door. It was not shame that guided him, it was stung passion; he wanted to share the closeness to Uncle Igor that came through the gift.

Breathless from the double taboo of what he was doing, violating boundaries and wearing women's clothes, he tried on the robe—and immediately threw it off, stunned by a nasty, longing sensation instigated by the vulgar deliberateness of transformation. However, the boy remembered the incident, the action, putting it away into a piggy bank as it were, with a premonition that it could come in handy.

The boy already understood how life worked in the City and had categorized all the people he knew. Fortunately the City's organization made it easy. In the center, behind a second Wall, was the Institute where his father worked. All the residents— guards, cleaning women, carpenters, drivers, scientists, shop clerks, teachers, doctors at the hospital, like his mother—served the Institute directly or indirectly.

Only Uncle Igor's role was unclear.

Not military, not civilian; none of the recognizable, tested types. Separate. Sui generis.

He was the only one who lived as if there were no City, Institute, Wall, commandant's office; no red flags, banners, demonstrations, posters calling for vigilance, or watchtowers.

The boy guessed that he did not see, did not know the main truth about Uncle Igor, which explained his special position. The boy could assume that Uncle Igor's work was secret, like his father's, for example. Or even more secret. But the point was that all the adults privy to secrets shared habits, jokes, and little words that Uncle Igor did not. Most important, they lived, like his father, with a sense of borrowed significance that gave them access, and they were afraid of losing it. Uncle Igor was on his own. The boy wanted that kind of unencumbered, independent fate for himself.

For Easter, Uncle Igor's table was laid with a long linen cloth embroidered with proverbs written in an old-fashioned script. On it stood a candelabrum for twelve candles and dark green shot glasses rimmed in gold. Uncle Igor took down an old guitar from the wall: the maker's mark glittered gold in a circle beneath the strings.

Uncle Igor, as small as a child—he needed a cushion on the chair—thin, with long gray hair, as luxurious as a woman's, in a gray jacket of fine wool and a white shirt, looked like an actor, a bit of a magician, who knew how to enliven things. The glasses and cutlery in the hands of his guests seemed to be drawing a design, creating something that they were unaware of, not realizing that they were merely stand-ins for another gathering.

Uncle Igor orchestrated the flow of conversation without any effort. The boy noticed how his father, usually unsociable, sat straighter and grew animated, how his mother grew lovelier, how the other guests relaxed, as if Uncle Igor were brushing them with a cheery gloss, an exciting glow, teaching them to appreciate once again the taste of food, the spiciness of spice and the saltiness of salt. Not a word about laboratories, state commissions, tests, aggregates, bonuses, formulas, equations, military acceptance, subcontractors—the adults didn't really know what else they could talk about, so their embarrassment was amusing, and they drank more wine or vodka. Uncle Igor played the guitar and sang songs that the boy had never encountered anywhere else, and then he turned on the record player, and dance melodies flew from the black lacquer records and spun in the air, so foreign that he thought he was hearing not music but the voice of the record itself composed of an unnatural, implausible substance.

Once the dancing began the children were sent off to play. That was what the boy had been waiting for. They played hide-and-seek, ever since he was little: only Uncle Igor's apartment had enough hiding places for them truly to hide and seek, for a long time and without giveaways.

The children were older now and kept up the old custom reluctantly, seemingly out of boredom. However, in fact, the game had a new meaning now: the boys listened to the girls' breathing, the girls hidden behind drapes, sometimes hopping in order to be found. In the dimly lit rooms, their first feelings arose. Only one room, at the far end of the corridor, was always locked.

The boy liked these hours of play. He hid better than the others, he could remain unnoticed in full view. The girls' silhouettes did not excite him; his lust was for something different.

The person hiding sees space inside out, with the eyes of subjects, walls, photographs. He tries to merge with the place, become part of it. For him, hide-and-seek was merely the prologue to a voyage, immersion in the attractive otherness, the life of and space inhabited by Uncle Igor.

He held his breath, surrounded by things that had lost their corporeality, had turned into velvet ghosts, that might speak in the dark, convey something tactile. The distant locked room did not interest him; he did not think that Uncle Igor could have literal secrets hidden behind the door. Besides, he did not want to uncover some part of his hidden life; he wanted to know his everyday existence, his dashing, undisguised freedom of action and opinion, his ability to live without fear, treat everyone independently and at the same time be needed and universally respected.

They played for a long time that evening. The thrill was gone. Hiding one more time, the boy noticed that the usually locked door was ajar, weak light coming through the crack.

The sudden sense that this was no accident made him catch his breath.

"I'll just peek in," the boy told himself. "Just a peek, that's all."

The desk lamp was on. Probably Uncle Igor or the help left it on and forgot to come back in the flurry of holiday preparations. Its light, so personal, secret, the setting of Uncle Igor's solitude and thoughts, beckoned irresistibly.

"I wasn't told not to go in here," thought the boy. "I'll say we were playing hide-and-seek. The door was ajar."

He walked around the room slowly, attentively looking at the cupboards, bookshelves, desk. A grandfather clock ticked loudly in the corner, marking the brief time he could spend here unnoticed.

He wanted to leave and took three steps toward the door; he grew anxious. He realized that all the books here were about chemistry. The same ones that his father had. But Uncle Igor had more books; his father knew only German and here there were volumes in English and French. The boy took one off the shelf— yes, the same stamp of the Institute library.

His father, when he worked at home, cleared his desk when he was done. If the boy needed to come into his room, he knocked first, and his father turned the work pages over. Uncle Igor left his desk as if he had walked out for a minute: tea in a glass, a viciously sharpened pencil on top of the pages. Typed pages, heavy honeycombs of formulas speckled with corrections.

The boy turned away. He felt a mix of disappointment and vague hope. Uncle Igor could not be his father's colleague. Yet he was. The books were evidence that he was merely a civil scientist, one of hundreds in the City.

Suddenly the boy noticed a small triangle of fabric that stuck out of the doors of the clothes closet, like the corner of a bookmark. Military green. With embroidered gold leaves. A sleeve, probably.

The boy pulled on the end but the doors were shut tight.

"I'll say that I wanted to hide in the closet," he decided. "They didn't forbid it."

The boy slowly opened the doors.

The bulb in the closet glowed like a treasure hunter's torch in a cave.

The gold embroidery blazed. The buttons were golden flashes. The orders shimmered in gold, scarlet, steel, and silver; the orders and stars made of blood-red enamel, the gray steel hammers and sickles, plows and bayonets, a soldier with a rifle; gold sheaves and leaves, the gold letters of *LENIN*.

A uniform hung in the closet. Covered in the heavy, round, scalelike discs of orders and medals from chest to navel. A major general's lonely big stars sparkled on the shoulder boards.

The uniform was small, almost a child's, just right for Uncle Igor. Without the awards it might have looked comical. But the golden, ruby, and sapphire reflections imbued it with supernatural might. The boy could not imagine what a man had to do to earn so many awards. Was he even a man? A hero? A higher being?

A cap on the shelf. Belt. A pair of boots.

A different Uncle Igor. The true one. Who had the right to a special life.

The boy had never seen such precious things up close. He ran his fingers over the gold, silver, and ruby scales, cold and heavy. The mirror on the inside of the door reflected a face made strange by confusion.

The uniform, hung with medals that seemed an integral part of it, radiated pure, absolute power. The boy could not control himself. He didn't think about being caught, punished, banished from Uncle Igor's house. He so wanted to commune with that power, feel himself inside it, that he took the uniform off the hanger and with an unexpected, agile move, as if stolen from the owner, slipped his arms into the sleeves.

His shoulders bent under the weight. You had to stand under the uniform as if under barbells at the gym. But the weight was inexpressibly pleasant, it both burdened and protected, it clad you in its thin silk lining.

The boy stood and did not recognize himself, as if he had put on not someone else's clothing but someone else's features and character. The embossed symbols he had internalized in childhood made him part of something immeasurably bigger, as vast as the starry sky.

He took a step toward the mirror. Blinded by the dazzling sparkle, he noticed the military emblems on the lapels almost accidentally.

Not tanks.

Not propellers.

Not crisscrossed artillery barrels.

Bowl and snake.

A golden bowl with a snake wrapped around it, its head raised as if to take a sip or to protect the forbidden vessel.

He had never seen an emblem like that. He didn't know what it meant.

In the midst of stars, sickles, hammers, and bayonets, the weapons of war and the weapons of labor welded into one, he thought, by the history of his country and therefore embossed on medals, the bowl and snake came from another, most ancient world when man was just beginning to name constellations. The boy suddenly understood that this inconspicuous and obscure symbol was the key; hidden, secret, it explained the orders, the general's rank, Uncle Igor's scientific path, combined it all into the secret of exclusivity, power, and strength.

The boy carefully took off the uniform and hung it back in the closet, leaving a corner of the sleeve sticking out between the doors. The obsession did not go away. Blessed heaviness. Complete protection.

He had found his idol. His path to becoming like Uncle Igor.

The bowl and snake.

Four years later the boy was the top student in chemistry. They were starting the last year of school. His father said that they would go see Uncle Igor to talk about the future. The boy guessed that his father, his kind father, milksop as his mother called him when she was angry, did not want him to repeat his path as the eternal number two, the reserve. His mother certainly did not want him to become a copy of her husband. They were prepared to give him to someone who knew how to forge destinies, change them for the better, higher, unattainable. The boy felt both rejection and joy. Their sacrifice was sweet to him. He knew now that the bowl and snake, the emblem of military medics, was just camouflage on Uncle Igor's uniform. He was not a physician. He did not invent medicines. Much in their City was not what it seemed, and as he grew up, the boy accepted it without embarrassment, with a readiness that surprised his parents.

He had expected a thorough interrogation and he was prepared to display his knowledge. But Uncle Igor asked a dozen rather simple questions, nodded, and said, "Fine, all right."

The boy felt Uncle Igor studying him. Looking at him absently, indifferently, weighing things that the boy did not know and could not imagine.

As they said good-bye in the hallways, Uncle Igor said casually, "I'll write a recommendation to the special faculty. But on one condition. Have him come tomorrow morning to the third entrance. I'll write a pass."

The parents and the boy were stunned.

The Institute's third entrance!

There were only three. Everyone in the City knew them.

The First had the wide gates for vehicles and battered turnstiles for the workers. There was a line of people waiting for passes, someone trying to use the hard-to-hear internal telephone. Documents were checked by fat-bellied paramilitary guards, revolvers in scuffed holsters, and it was all redolent of boredom, sweat, and cabbage soup from the canteen.

His father went through the Second entrance to go to work. Heavy billowing blinds covered the Institute's glass vestibule, and it was only when the doors opened for an instant that you could see the gray marble lobby and the guards in gray suit jackets. The cardboard passes accepted at the First were not valid here. They had to be like his father's: with a photograph and in a dark leatherette case.

The Third . . . The Third was a metal door with a bell. A door in the brick end of the building without windows. Somehow everyone knew that it led to the same place as the other two: into the inner perimeter of the Institute, a city in the City. No parking was allowed opposite the Third, a traffic officer came over instantly. No buildings over two stories could be built next to it.

But no one knew to whom the Third entrance belonged, who met visitors at the door. The ones who did know didn't talk.

"The Second," his father either asked or corrected.

"No. The Third," Uncle Igor replied with a gentle smile. "At eleven."

The boy felt that answer cut the ties that connected him to his parents. His father had not been past the door of the Third. He couldn't dream of being there. But he would be.

Tomorrow.

At eleven.

In the morning, his father gave him his watch. The boy wanted the whole world to know where he was going. But there weren't many pedestrians, and the street was completely empty by the Third entrance. If only someone would look out a window or out of the passing bus!

The second hand made him hurry. The boy put his finger on the bell. Pressed. The button was rigid and immobile. Silence. Suddenly he imagined that he could still turn around and go;

back to his mother and father, to his previous life. He looked around. A dusty street. A tall tramp in a dirty, black padded jacket stopped on the corner and was looking at him; where did he come from, this was the City, there were no tramps here! The boy pushed the bell as hard as he could. A harsh ring like an alarm sounded inside.

A grumpy and surprised ensign took his new passport and copied his name. He moved a yellow notebook with curling edges toward him: Sign in. He called on the phone, dialing two numbers: 2-8.

Another ensign came and said, Follow me. He had the bowl and snake in his buttonhole. The boy's heart pounded at the discreet proximity of the secret. Hallway. A door padded with oilcloth. A narrow passage through the courtyard with a brick wall; whining behind it. Could it be dogs? The next door. Worn linoleum on the floor. The smell of a classroom not cleaned after vacation. Windows with a view of high brick walls. A labyrinth. He felt a chill. He was lost in space, he could no longer figure out where the street was.

A safe door. A big empty room. Marks on the wallpaper showed where shelves had been. The boy was confused and depressed. Where was the equipment, where was the laboratory, where was the secret?

Uncle Igor in a plain blue lab coat came through the door opposite. Yet another different Uncle Igor. He beckoned with two fingers: Follow me. A long, dark, dusty corridor brought them to the dressing room with wide metal lockers for clothing and to one side, a shower room, the showerheads the size of sunflowers.

"Once, we used to change here," Uncle Igor said. "The clean zone begins from here. Now this place no longer exists. On paper this wing has been razed to build a new one. But the builders are late. This place does not exist, understand? That's why I could bring you here."

The boy stood listening to every word.

"Your father is a good chemist," Uncle Igor said. "But he is afraid of what he's researching. Afraid. That's why I will never take him into my laboratory. Are you afraid?"

"No," he replied without thinking.

"Open the end one," Uncle Igor said pointing to the lockers.

The boy opened it. Something lay inside, squashed between the locker walls: a green rubber skin grafted to a gas mask. He pulled it out, extremely heavy, slippery with talcum powder, resembling the scales of a snakeskin shed years ago.

"Put it on," Uncle Igor said.

He managed to get his legs into the rubber pants and pulled on the suit. The tight stiff collar constricted his throat. The cuffs were tight on his wrists. Breathing was hard and a fog appeared before his eyes. Uncle Igor's hands straightened his back and closed the seam along the spine, tied the straps on his ankles—and he found himself inside a rubber womb, a live infant in the body of a dead reptile.

"Turn around. Look in the mirror." Uncle Igor's voice seemed far away.

He moved clumsily, as if learning to walk, shuffling the unwieldy boots. He desperately wanted to be out of the rubber womb and its slippery, deadening embrace.

"Look at yourself," Uncle Igor repeated out of the depths.

Through the fogged lenses of the mask he made out the mirror.

A monster looked at him. A horrible swamp creature with dull round eyes, mouthless, faceless, alien to every living thing, with no resemblance or relation to anything.

It was him. A different him.

Special. Unrecognizable.

Suddenly the boy felt the unknown peace, the highest protection that the suit bestowed on him.

The rubber folds no longer squeezed him. His throat got used to the collar's hold. The boy stood without sensing the many kilograms of rubber weight, he seemed to be floating. The thing in the mirror was he, and he did not want the merging to end. This was more thrilling than Uncle Igor's medal-laden uniform, more exciting than anything he had ever felt.

In that outfit he feared nothing. Like Uncle Igor.

When the boy climbed out, sweaty, reddened, smeared with talcum and a slippery paste, completely happy, Uncle Igor smiled broadly and slapped him on the shoulder.

"That's our old suit. We began with those. Go now, they'll see you out. I'll write the recommendation. If you graduate with honors, I'll hire you."

He froze, he couldn't believe it. Uncle Igor gently shoved his wet back: Go, go.

CHAPTER 4

Lieutenant Colonel Shershnev took the day off. He was on his way to celebrate his son's birthday. Sixteen. Last year in school.

His wife had divorced him after his third tour in Chechnya, when Maxim was three. Now she was remarried and Maxim had a stepsister. Shershnev tried to believe that the war had broken them up. The usual officer's story, he wasn't the first or the last. There had been a lot of divorces in his unit in those years. The country lived as if there were no battles on its territory. His wife, Shershnev kept telling himself, had joined the majority that did not want to know about blood and mud, the military and the victims.

Yet he had not been able to convince himself completely, and this worried Shershnev, who could not tolerate ambiguity.

He did not regret what he had done in that war—or the following ones.

There was only one incident that Shershnev considered—well, probably wrong, fraught. He couldn't find better words. Wrong, not in the moral sense, his conscience didn't bother him. Speaking only of morality, he would have acted the same way again. Yet he sensed some kind of violation then, some twist of fate, that predetermined—not directly—his wife's departure and the gradual loss of contact with his son, who had transformed, it seemed to Shershnev, into an alien, thin-boned, wishy-washy breed.

Marina was overly sensitive, to the point of divination; she could guess something out of thin air and convey it consciously or not to their son. She did not forbid them from seeing each other; on the contrary, she sometimes asked him to come by and spend the day with Maxim. But Shershnev sensed that his son was not simply separating from him because he was growing older; he seemed to know something he should not about his father and seemed to be asking, looking for an argument, insults: Who are you really, Father? What is your true face? What did you do in the war?

Shershnev categorically rejected the idea that he had something to be ashamed of. He considered his conscience clear.

Yet he returned dozens of times to that night, to that shipping container in the back of the military base that served as a cell and interrogation room. He remembered the smell of blood and vomit; one of his colleagues joked that the enemy's vomit and shit smelled different. Dim light, a naked man in a gas mask handcuffed to the wall.

Repeated questions: who, when, where. Screams, whispers, curses, cries, moans.

Lieutenant Evstifeyev, squeezing the air hose leading to the mask.

The familiar feeling of power: turning the prisoner into a nameless dummy with a faceless rubber head, forcing the naked body, open to suffering, to respond to the rhythmic and inexorable language of pain: who, where, when? The freedom of not hiding their faces, multiplying the power, making it profoundly personal and thus particularly intense and intoxicating.

Now Shershnev searched his memory for another exit from the container, from its four metal walls. He was not repenting, he didn't care about the torture, the squashed fingers, broken ribs, and eyes bulging from suffocation behind the murky glass of the gas mask.

But he should have guessed, was obligated to guess right away that the agent was merely using them to do his dirty work. Shershnev had spent a long time looking for the field commander he was ordered to destroy. One of the agents pointed to the commander's alleged messenger. In fact, he gave Shershnev a nobody, a teenager who knew nothing, drunk on hatred for the soldiers; he was the last male in a clan that was feuding with the agent's clan.

But Shershnev fell for it, impermissibly caught up in the heat of the hunt, and believed, he believed that the prisoner, just a kid, knew where the commander was.

It was all in vain. Their stubborn torture. His adolescent, ritual pride that would not let him admit he was not the one.

Their meager inventiveness.

His patience with being a victim.

When he finally broke and spoke freely, Shershnev instantly understood whom he had allowed to fool him.

They could have tried to save the kid. Given or sold him to the relatives who stood at the gates of the base day and night, handing over worn lists, compiled by unknown people. This was a procedure with secondary prisoners—they gave a lot more money for a live one than a corpse.

But Shershnev ordered them to kill the boy and bury him in the secret pit behind the cement plant. The mistake was much too shameful.

It was a good thing that Evstifeyev was a dull and obedient chump; he didn't seem to have understood a thing. If the boy had talked, both the locals and his colleagues would have heard. Rumors spread quickly here.

The military could arrest anyone and beat a confession out of them; that was in the nature of things. But an officer who fell as stupidly as Shershnev had for the agent's trick would have turned into a jerk for his men and a laughingstock for others; his authority would vanish in the blink of an eye.

Shershnev did not wait for the execution of his order. He left. When he returned in a week's time, he asked Sergeant Mishustin, drunkard, fornicator, executioner, and trader in prisoners—Is it done?—and received the expected answer, Yeah, it's done, it's done, cap.

Mishustin could permit himself to be offhand with senior officers. He handled financial affairs of generals, whose multitude of stars made the four Shershnev had earned as a captain seem pale by comparison.

Shershnev could not punish the agent who had set him up. He did not work just for Shershnev. And he wasn't merely an informant, he was the product of a lengthy period of time spent in the limbo of war, where he had fought for both sides, and he had set up an illicit business—and there could be no other—with the army; and now a good position, albeit not in the top ranks, was in the offing for him in Chechnya's new administration. The agent naturally said nothing about how he had tricked the captain; he did not want the boy's family to learn who had turned him in to the federal troops.

So Shershnev was left with blood shed in vain. With fanaticism that had served nothing. With the feeling that he had been stupid in the heat of the hunt, taken down a puppy instead of a wolf, shamed himself before the whole world. He had carried out a heavy and expensive fatal torture on a youth who was worth a kopeck.

There were men in his unit who would not have understood Shershnev's worries; they would have said, one more, one less, who cares. Shershnev would have forgiven himself for missing the mark. But knowing how to aim, yet not knowing how to distinguish targets, was inexcusable.

Evstifeyev died six months later. He was hit by machine gun fire from a cellar during a search. Mishustin was killed by outsiders or friends when he took a batch of corpses to the cement factory. Shershnev didn't consider this particularly coincidental. War is war. He did feel a secret relief when he learned from his colleagues that the unwitting witnesses to his mistake were dead—Mishustin was a busybody, he knew everything and everyone, and he must have realized how cleverly the agent had screwed the captain.

A month after his return home, Marina told him she was pregnant.

Shershnev had known various nights with her. He could tell, it seemed to him, what was happening during sex beyond the sex itself, what other meanings carnal love could have.

He especially remembered one night, actually a late summer evening. They had gone mushroom picking in the countryside that morning; people were selling baskets of young agaric by the metro entrance. They found very few, the locals who got up early had cut them all down. Ferns were bruised and trampled around tree stumps and the cut mushroom stems showed white in the moss.

They did have the river, the swaying rope bridge, swimming in the rushing water, unexpectedly warm and silvered from surface to bottom with the flickering schools of fish. The day was bigger, more expansive, more important than other days. When they made love that evening, he sensed that on such days, under a special sign, beloved God-sent children were conceived.

Then Marina skipped a period, a bodily echo, a light flutter of the universe. But the test was negative. Soon after he left on his first mission, which made him forget the bridge and the river and the embrace.

The night of his return was poisoned by the pathetic, sexless nakedness that Shershnev had seen in the container. Without caresses or tenderness. He was desperate to come, as if to pour out into his wife everything that had happened to him; he did not notice that Marina was moaning with pain, not pleasure.

Then Shershnev once again started getting used to his wife's vulnerable body, given in to his power; they made love over and over, finding themselves as they had been. But he knew that Maxim had been conceived that very first, very dark night.

Yesterday Maxim had turned sixteen. Shershnev offered to take him and his friends to the country, to roast shashlik over a campfire, hoping that Maxim would appreciate it. But his son asked for a paintball match in a location he had selected.

Shershnev said yes and rented a bus. Marina and her new husband were against it, worrying about injuries. That was the only reason why he had agreed. He didn't like the idea much. Maxim knew that his father was in the army, that he had been in real wars. But they never talked about it; not even the little that Shershnev had the right to tell.

He did not tie his son's fate with the fate of that now name-less man tossed into the pit at the cement plant. However, the coincidence—one man died and Maxim was called into life—seemed too obvious to be ignored.

And now Maxim wanted to play at war. Why? What for? Shershnev sensed in this request a bad convergence of two worlds that he superstitiously preferred to keep apart. Even if the bullets in the paintball guns were toys. His colleagues, who knew a thing or two about his family problems, were pleased: at last the boy is showing guts, the father's genes dominating. You'll play together. But Shershnev was certain that Maxim would ask him to play for the other side.

He had explained everything he had done as being done for Maxim: for the sake of his peaceful life. Shershnev could not admit that his son was important and necessary to him only as a justification. Now he was expecting some vengeful trick, a rico-chet from the past.

But he could not refuse.

Seeing the billboard—*Territory X, Paintball*—Shershnev turned off the highway. He did not have time before the trip to study where exactly they were going. Probably an abandoned ware-house or an old sanatorium turned into the stage set of a battlefield (ridiculous to those who know) or a postnuclear apocalypse world.

Shershnev had seen Grozny after two army attacks. The sub-urbs of Damascus bombed into rubble. Burned villages. He had the arrogant superiority of a man whose entire biography from school to military service had trained him to see violence as the source of experience, to respect its authenticity, its true and indelible traces.

He looked in the rearview mirror at his son and his son's friends. Fledglings. Small fry. Tadpoles. He felt the urge to rub their noses in real ash and mud, to turn off the road to find not a suburban, well-trodden park, but an eviscerated village with no life, no transparent neighborly secrets, because all the doors were smashed, curtains torn down, closets emptied, and every crack checked by the eyes of soldiers.

The hassle of the depopulated village elicited, dragged into the light, the mean and persistent feeling of a well-planned raid. How many times had they driven up like this, in the early years only in armored cars and later in buses, checking their weapons, preparing to surround and break in! He had felt the essence, the rhythm of that feeling in a poem that a dedicated old man read to them in their military English classes—a teacher who had known the legendary era of the Cambridge Five. Poetry usually did not interest Shershnev. Poetry had been punishment in school, collapsing in his memory like mush; he couldn't understand why people wrote it, why they had this bizarre fancy. But this poem— the only one in his life—he memorized without repetition, for it fell so perfectly on the contours of his soul. And now he muttered it, glad that he could find his own feelings in the sounds of a foreign tongue:

O what is that sound which so thrills the ear
Down in the valley drumming, drumming?

Only the scarlet soldiers, dear,
The soldiers coming.

O what is that light I see flashing so clear
Over the distance brightly, brightly?
Only the sun on their weapons, dear,
As they step lightly.

He wanted to continue, but stopped. They had arrived.

The paintball grounds were in a former Pioneer camp.

Shershnev hoped that they would not be playing among shipping containers. One time he and his colleagues had gone there to relax and found the paintball grounds had been set up in imitation of a battle in a port. Cheap and easy, you just collect a lot of old containers for the price of scrap metal, set them up in an empty field, and you have your labyrinth. The owners told them that lots of people do this, it's the cheapest way—the main expense is renting the land. His colleagues, who had been in that war, laughed, banging their rifle butts against the ribbed sides—the containers were hollow, empty; Shershnev enjoyed that feeling of common experience that should not be spoken aloud. But he did not want to play with Maxim in that setting.

He arranged for a different paintball battlefield.

A Pioneer camp. Recognizable, typical. Shershnev was in one like that as a child—on the territory of his father's garrison. A booth at the gate. One-story buildings for units, painted with yellow whitewash that could be scraped off, dissolved in water, and turned into a spotting liquid to splash one another from old food cans. A parade ground, overgrown with grass, and flagpoles.

A bust of Lenin, covered in silver caustic paint. A low brick bath-house. Flower beds made of tires in front of the administration building. Loudspeakers on poles . . .

He smelled smoke—there were campfires in the distance, to create a battle atmosphere. Maxim went to the office, because he wanted to pay for the match himself, albeit with his father's money. His friends waited by the bus. Shershnev thought that they would light up, but no one smoked. He was the only one with a cigarette, he took a drag and exhaled, chasing away a bad premonition as he looked at two layers, two periods in his memory.

Here he is, commander of the Pioneer squad. They were playing Lightning Strike, which they waited for all day; they were crawling under cover of the crookedly shorn shrubs toward the headquarters of the "Blues" in building 12, and they could hear their general, Pioneer commander Venya Valkov, giving orders. Shershnev's team was anticipating running inside, pulling off the blue scraps sewn onto the enemy's shirts, and the opponents would have to sit on the floor, seething with anger, right where they were "killed."

And here—overwhelming—were the same asphalt paths, neglected shrubs, yellow buildings, and redbrick steam bath. The stands with red-and-white slogans were riddled with bullets and burned. A homemade banner with a snarling wolf hung on the flagpole. The same camp, the same sign in a tight arc over the gate: *YOUNG LENINIST.* The woodland was different, not sparse pine but thickly planted deciduous trees, distorted, twisted by the inner gravitation of the mountains. Nearby flowed a turbulent mountain river, and its noise was akin to the voices of the people who had taken over the camp: as if someone had gathered the most alien, piercing sounds and fused them into one.

He was the unit commander, a small group. His job now was to observe, because everything had already been predetermined; the treated prayer beads in a carved casket, the beads of roughly polished wood, for wood absorbed aromatic oils so well, covering up the faint scent of the special substance.

Shershnev was surprised when they let him see the plan the higher-ups had developed. He said carefully that it would be easier to point a rocket or strike from helicopters. He did not want to risk his men on an operation for somebody's scientific degrees, for the sake of field tests of a prehistoric weapon that smacked of theatrical farce—they might as well ask them to shoot arrows or use daggers. But now he literally sensed the movement of beads in the casket, anticipated someone's hands opening the box and taking out the beads strung on rough thread, the false gift; they would be running the beads between their fingers, which would be followed by a shrill scream that did not know a man's shame.

When the man who had the same name as the boy he had tortured, his long-sought enemy, the field commander, and in the recent past, chairman of the Dawn Kolkhoz, Shershnev's age, cried out his pain, the major raised a prayer, pagan, fierce, blasphemous, to the Maker—the maker of that imperceptible death imbued in the prayer beads.

He was awarded an order and a promotion. But after that they did not so much hold him back as set him aside, like an instrument that justified its tricky shape but was rarely needed. Others were sent on ordinary assignments and there were no more operations in that special line. In any case, in their section.

Other men slowly but surely passed him in rank, awards, and informal ratings of operatives. His career was marked by the mysterious substance about which he knew nothing, even though he had to sign a separate nondisclosure agreement along with the usual ones before the raid. Somewhere up high secret plans were conceived and orders given. Somewhere in the laboratories of their departments, thought Shershnev, chemists were still creating substances. The lieutenant colonel waited for the moment when they would be in sync: order and substance, he and the next target.

Shershnev finished his smoke, stamped out the butt. The decision came on its own: today he would let his son shoot him. Not kill but wound. It was necessary. Let Maxim see the paint blood on his father's body and feel joy and embarrassment. That red spot, that successful shot would be their first adult story that they would later recall—how skillfully I got you, oh, yes, how you did.

Shershnev pulled on the game coveralls. The teams split up. One was to storm "base"—an old unit dorm—and the other defend it. Shershnev joined the attacking side. They would have more losses. He wanted to say something to his son, but while he was thinking of the right words, Maxim shut the visor of his helmet and gave him a two-fingered V for victory sign.

Once again Shershnev lay behind trees, looking at yellow houses. He crawled, shot, commanded his subordinates—left, right, go around. Of course, he was playing at a third, a quarter of his strength, missing on purpose or even skipping a shot. He could have shot everyone here in ten minutes, even with the clumsy paintball rifle that did not shoot accurately or far. But he played around, trying to overcome the years of training and know-how, trying to force himself to make the wrong response. Shershnev looked for Maxim, he thought he might have seen him in the window, his helmet number 1. They all had the same uniform and helmets, and he worried he would make a mistake and let one of his players "kill" or "wound" his son; he stealthily steered the game in the direction he wanted.

The defenders retreated into the building. Shershnev ran over and threw himself over a windowsill. He wanted to reach his son unharmed, reducing his team along the way, so that Maxim's victory would be even more impressive.

But it turned out that the narrow corridors were piled with metal beds, tables, and chairs. This was hard even for him. Without noticing, Shershnev had gotten into the rhythm and rage of action. He dropped one with a precise shot right in the visor, which was then covered with red. He got another with a round across the legs. The responding shot hit the wall by his head.

As a distraction, Shershnev threw a desk into the corridor. Then he jumped out. In his peripheral vision, he saw motion in an empty room. He shot a round, at close range, knowing that the paintballs really hurt at that distance but unable to stop himself. He struck as he would in real combat, from below, vertically from groin to neck, then ran two steps to finish him off, pointed the barrel . . .

No shot.

The paintball rifle had fewer shells in the magazine than his habitual automatic gun.

The number one was painted on the player's helmet. Maxim, thrown onto his back, smeared with fake blood, groaned and tried to crawl away, pushing his feet on the slippery linoleum.

The paint had splashed lightly on the plastic visor. Eyes wild with pain and fear stared out at him.

Shershnev could have made it all right. He could have knelt. Embraced him, held him close. Asked forgiveness. Explained what had happened to him, that it was a bad idea to play paintball with a professional soldier. But the same evil force that directed his finger on the trigger and readily responded to a march—"Only the scarlet soldiers, dear, The soldiers coming"—that force turned Shershnev around and away. His son couldn't whine like that, couldn't be so afraid. And most importantly, he could not, did not have the right to look at his father that way.

Shershnev went into the corridor. There were no opponents left. He won the skirmish he had wanted to lose.

His phone vibrated silently in the pocket of his overalls.

"You? Tomorrow, eight o'clock at the Directorate. Got it? Over."

CHAPTER 5

The doctors at the hospital treated Kalitin with extreme respect. It wasn't because of his expensive insurance. The doctors considered Kalitin a former colleague and at first expected him to be demanding. But he turned out to be an ideal patient: he wasn't worried, he didn't ask questions, he didn't call the duty nurse at night, and he patiently dealt with the procedures.

They thought that he was not afraid.

Kalitin was afraid. The way he had been afraid only once in his life, during a long childhood winter. They had just moved to the City, where they were assigned a two-room apartment with kitchen and bath—it had seemed enormous to him after the small room in a communal flat. He went to a new school—where everyone was a newbie like him, and there were no huge second-grade and third-grade bullies, as there had been at the old school. Life seemed radiant and invigorating.

Suddenly something inexplicable happened to his mother and father. In the evenings, his parents placed a pot over the telephone—they had their own phone now—and shut themselves up in the kitchen. The water poured full-blast into the sink and the radio proclaimed loudly and solemnly: Today the entire country... Their voices could barely be heard: strange, aloof. He hid in the hallway behind his grandmother's ancient, molting fur coat, trying to catch even a word.

His mother was a surgeon. Just recently she had told them proudly how well equipped her new operating theater was. Now she wanted to leave urgently. His father was trying to convince her to stay.

"You have my last name," he said softly.

"You think they don't have my personnel file?" she replied.

"It will be all right," he said uncertainly. "Look, they made me a senior fellow. They gave me access. First category! Do you think I would have that if they suspected us of anything? Apartment. Salary. Rations. They approved my dissertation topic."

"Have you read what they're writing in the papers?" she asked bitterly. "Killer doctors! I studied with one of them, don't you understand?"

His father stopped talking. Then he said: "Igor will help."

"As long as Igor doesn't fall himself," she replied joylessly, dully. "This is just the beginning."

Those nocturnal words destroyed the invisible, warm softness that was his home, leaving gaping holes open to uncertainty and fear. He began to think that some of the teachers regarded him strangely: as if they knew something. Fear became the spice in meals, the shadow of all feelings, the echo of all sounds. Fear took out all the bannisters and supports from the world, stole his usual sense of balance, took away his agility.

That's why he fell in the locker room after gym class. He got tangled in his trousers. He clumsily knocked over someone's canvas bag from the bench. A change of clothing fell out—and a deck of greasy photographs with torn, chewed edges.

Vovka Sapozhok, the class clown, hurried over and looked over his shoulder; he whistled in astonishment and then gave a salacious, disgusting smack of his lips.

The cards scattered, mixed up. Naked arms, breasts, buttocks, black-and-white glossy flesh, stockings, ostrich feathers, gauzy curtains, sofas, slippers. Women on their backs, crouching, kneeling. Naked men in black hats. Dark thickets of hair between plump female thighs. Penises in mouths. The nakedness was not of the bodies, but of the secret real life of men and women, covered by clothing, the frightening seriousness of what was taking place in the photos, it was like seeing birth or death. And strange, bizarre apparel, jewelry, belonging to a fairy tale theater, a foreign ritual, an extinct world.

He looked, frozen in place. Sapozhok grew quiet and bent forward, leaning on his shoulder as if in love.

Voices burst into the dressing room. Senior students, the volleyball team. Tall, sweaty, angry after the game. Sapozhok was first to sense danger and tried to jump away, but fell on his friend's back, humping like a street dog, a hurrying runt, and then rolled off and vanished.

The older boys laughed and guffawed loudly and then suddenly stopped.

"You little rat." A heavy blow knocked the boy toward the bench.

The boy knew that voice. The son of Colonel Izmailov, the City's military commandant. He had seen him with his father at Uncle Igor's house. He overheard the adults talking about how after the war the colonel had been sent to Germany to disassemble scientific equipment and came back with "a lot of interesting things for himself personally."

Interesting. The boy realized that Izmailov junior had taken those dirty pictures from his father. Secretly of course. And if they were found, if a teacher walked in right . . .

He wet himself.

Izmailov picked him up by the scruff of his neck. The pictures were no longer on the floor.

Dark, round-headed, the commandant's son looked at him but was also looking around furtively—apparently he didn't trust everyone on the team. And the smaller kids were nearby as well.

"You spill this to anyone, I'll kill you, you little shit!" Izmailov shoved him into the corner of the room.

Even before, when there was peace in the family, the boy would not have told his parents anything. How could he prove that he had not wanted them and had not intended to steal those cards? How could he admit that he had seen them at all?

Now the boy felt that even if he did confess—his parents would not listen to him, wouldn't condescend to that.

They had no time for him.

During the following week, Izmailov "accidentally" ran into the boy three times at the classroom door. He just stood there and looked at him. His gaze was beginning to show his father's stern nature; he could sit calmly at the table, looking around courteously at his fellow diners, and people would clam up, lay down their forks, and start rubbing the stems of their vodka glasses for some reason. The boy recalled the black-and-white bodies, submissively bent, the men in black top hats, Izmailov's hand, his angry hot whisper, and felt that he did not have the strength to rid himself of that memory.

Then the day came when once again gym class coincided with volleyball practice. Earlier he would have managed to get out of it, for example, by eating snow to catch cold and staying home. But he couldn't manage it. It required a little bit of strength on hand, you couldn't borrow it, for that sort of ploy. The boy was tormented by fear and guilt: if he had not knocked over Izmailov's bag, nothing would have happened.

He sat through the class. Put on skis that were too long and poorly waxed and had loose mounts for his gym period.

Cross-country.

He did the first lap with enjoyment, surprised by his body's indifference, its dumb and uncomplaining skill despite the splintery skis and the horror ahead. The wind came up and the light frost grew even lighter, and the snow on the course, even though it was rolled and compacted, started sticking to the badly waxed skis.

A raw blizzard started. The whirling whiteness hid the figures of his classmates and the school building. Snow formed a tight hump on his right ski; the boy jerked his foot and the screws pulled out of the loose holes, with a spray of rusty wood particles.

He stood there, one foot with a ski, one without. He realized that there was no goodness in life that would save him from Izmailov waiting in the locker room; the knowledge was as obvious and final as a sentence; very adult. The boy prayed wordlessly, begging the blizzard, the sky, anyone—save me!

The world, it seemed, did not respond.

He took off the second ski and meekly headed for the gym.

There was no one on the stoop. The volleyball net was still swaying gently. A whistle lay on the referee's stool. The ball had rolled into a corner.

It felt as if he had walked through some dangerous hole in the blizzard and ended up in an alternative world, without people. If a war had started, there would have been air raid sirens wailing throughout the City. Had the enemy attacked suddenly?

He peeked into the cafeteria. Glasses of tea and unfinished pieces of bread on the tables. He could smell scorched buckwheat porridge. The old cat, Duska, sat by the trash can for bones and peels.

The door to the auditorium was slightly open. He could hear stifled sobs.

It was dark in the auditorium, just a few lights were on. It was filled with teachers, students, guards, and cooks. The director was on the stage. He raised his only hand, as if trying to catch someone flying away, and in the same voice he used when he had sent his tank battalion into attack, shouted:

"The moment of silence is over! On your knees! On your knees!" He knelt first, and everyone followed.

"Let us remember," the director's voice broke. "Let us remember . . . Our dear—" The old crooked scar that went across his temple and cheek turned white and his face was suffused with bad blood. An old concussion, a German shell striking the tank turret, deafened him once again, he sank to the floor, while a simple-hearted cook cried out:

"They killed him!"

Everyone started to cry, the words released the cries.

Someone put a hand on his shoulder. Izmailov. His mouth was twisted and there were tears in his empty, wild eyes. The boy felt that he was crying, too. Izmailov got up and wandered off. People stood up, holding on to one another, stunned.

A portrait of a man with a mustache hung in the middle of the stage. The boy knew the City had been founded on his direct orders. The portrait had a black ribbon draped across one corner.

Believing in this man's immortality, in his name's immortality, the boy could not accept that he was actually dead, that he was reduced to a body emptied of its spirit. He thought that he had not really died, but had merely sacrificed himself for an hour, a day, in order to stop Izmailov's revenge, to save him, the most insignificant of the insignificant. He was engulfed by an uncontrollable wave of happiness and pain, the desire to sacrifice himself in return, to give his entire life, present and future, to the benevolent power embodied in that familiar, comforting portrait. He sobbed passionately, discharging the fear, and the ceiling flipped upside down and the lamps flew in a tight arc.

Darkness. Serenity.

The sharpness of smelling salts.

Izmailov no longer approached him. At the end of the summer, he disappeared from the City. Along with the commandant father.

His parents no longer locked themselves in the kitchen in the evening or covered the telephone with a pot. His mother started praising her new operating theater again.

"They removed Izmailov," Uncle Igor said with marked indifference, when they came to visit. "He turned out to be an accomplice of Beria, that enemy of the people."

The boy thought that this was all orchestrated by the benevolent power that he had managed to reach. He now knew that the man with the face in the portrait had in fact died; died forever. However, he divined the presence of the same power in Uncle Igor; in his simple, radiant word "removed," which obscured his triumph; the covert, great knowledge of causes and effects.

At the hospital, the same childish fear of inferiority and abandonment gnawed at him.

But now there was no more saving strength. All its mirages had vanished, like the banners and heraldry of the country where he had been born.

What was left was a patient's obedience. And thoughts in which he tried to rationalize his fear and find the path to and support for an unconditional hope, and not an illusory one.

Kalitin set aside the newspaper. He did not like reading on a screen, his eyes tired too quickly, and he had made reading newspapers part of his self-image: the conservative scientist, an émigré who could not reach previously attained heights in his historical homeland and retired.

He also had an instinctive fear of computers and smartphones that collected and saved metadata; he tried not to use search engines that remembered your questions; he did not trust VPN protocols or encryption.

Just an anonymous print paper; a fresh edition, bought at a kiosk.

Now the newspapers were brought to him by hospital staff, who joked respectfully about the lonely old man: Who else could leaf so calmly through the hysterical pages of news while he knew there was a suspicion of inoperable cancer and that at any moment the test results and final diagnosis would be revealed?

A chemist by education, Kalitin knew a lot about the human body, but only from a narrow and specific point of view: how to kill the body. He had a fairly good idea of modern methods of treating cancer, some of which were distantly related to his research; after all, on some level he had studied the directed destruction of specific cells.

But he remained ignorant in medicine. His academic, theoretical thoughts about death and his routine closeness to it in the laboratory gave Kalitin the perverted arrogance of a technocrat who believes that destruction and creation, killing and healing were equally possible; anything that could be broken could be fixed—thing, body, spirit—it was the job of other specialists who would be at hand when needed: repairmen, doctors, psychologists.

He who developed substances from which there was no salvation, who knew the effect of their virulent molecules, still believed childishly that salvation was always possible in the case of an ordinary illness, it was just a question of timely intervention, a question of means, effort, and price; Kalitin was prepared to pay the highest price.

He could afford a good hospital. Good doctors. But that was not enough for firm hope. It would be stupid to expect help. They let him know that more than once. The invitation to consult the investigative group was a farewell gesture, a perfunctory administrative kindness. They knew or guessed that most likely he would be gone in a year. National frugality: squeeze the last of the toothpaste from the tube. He had to work off the hospital bills, balance the debit-credit, for his insurance would not cover everything. And then there was the funeral.

They didn't tell him over the phone which crime the group was investigating. Secrecy. Not over the phone. What do they know about secrecy? In his ancient past, an armed messenger would come to Kalitin with a sealed envelope in a sealed pouch. Secrecy... As if he couldn't guess since it was all over the newspapers. Anaphylactic shock or its simulation. It was probably a substance of natural origins. Not his lab, not his work. In a restaurant, at close distance. Before witnesses. Risky. He didn't die right away, he held on, whispered. Distance? Dose? Method? Weather? Specific information on the organism? Food? Incidentally, it wasn't clear whether he had time to eat or not, what he had eaten didn't interest the press at all, and there wasn't a word about alcohol, the stupid fools. Interesting, interesting ... He had to read about it some more.

In the first few years after his defection, Kalitin had not read any newspapers. The news did not interest him. The laboratory, his baby, was back there in his homeland that betrayed him. Research was frozen and the staff given unpaid vacation.

He had hoped that they would believe him here and give him resources and colleagues. He would restore his arsenal and continue his interrupted research. Special services, Kalitin told himself, were the same everywhere. Certainly former enemies from the other side of the Iron Curtain, who had to collect information on his laboratory grain by grain and who had seen his creations at work—they would understand what goods he was bringing: excellent, with prospects, invaluable.

Interrogations, checks. His fate was decided slowly, with difficulty, but he waited and hoped. They scraped him clean, got everything out of him—except for Neophyte, his last secret; a substance that was not yet fully documented. Kalitin also did not tell them about what they called testing on dummies in his laboratory.

In the end, they gave him the chance to stay. They hid him from the bloodhounds. But they gave him an insignificant, albeit very well-paid, job as an outside consultant in investigations dealing with chemical weapons.

It was like rubbing his nose in it: you made the mess, you clean it up.

Kalitin tried hinting again that he could resume his work.

They promised to try him in that case.

It was only then that he realized they were handling him carefully, like a chemically dangerous substance, like a contaminated site. They put him in isolation so that no one could find and use him. In the end, it was much cheaper to pay him a salary and keep him under control than to fight the monsters he could create all over the world.

So he had received the desired recognition from his former enemies: they knew his value and that was why they put him under lock and key. They seemed to understand—and there had been psychologists among the interviewers—that he had been capable of making a break only once in his life, and he used it up, would never try again.

He relaxed and accepted the painful and impossible.

In 1991 he had just a few months left to complete the synthesis and prepare his best creation for testing. The most stable, the most untraceable substance. Neophyte. To create not an experimental version but a balanced composition ready for production.

For many years that ideal eluded him. But Kalitin overcame all obstacles, solved scientific puzzles, obtained increased financing. He felt that the birth of the desired higher substance could no longer be stopped, that it was as inevitable as sunrise.

Of course, the administrative organism was already sick, falling apart as if the country had been poisoned. Delays in equipment. Delays in salaries. The uncertainty of the bosses. The unnoticeable van disguised as a bread truck stopped coming with its delivery of dummies from the prison. He needed another three, two, even just one.

Kalitin had nothing of his own. They delivered everything to him, extracting it from the bowels of the earth, gathering it at factories, if necessary buying it for hard currency abroad; if they couldn't buy it, they stole it, copied it, or manufactured a single device at an experimental factory at unbelievable cost.

Suddenly this horn of plenty that covered every possible register and classification from bolts and wires to rare isotopes stopped working. Dried up.

Worst of all, Kalitin no longer felt the directing and demanding will of the state in the people who had always been his trusted connections.

Even when the Party had declared perestroika and glasnost, they had laughed and assured him that the changes would not affect their industry. Now the bosses vacillated and started conversations on conversion and disarmament, unheard of in the past.

Kalitin remembered the day they told him the work would stop temporarily: allegedly they had to resolve issues of the laboratory's administrative subordination.

For the first time in his life, he felt that there existed something higher than him, higher than the laws of chemistry and physics, which he learned to understand and use. Kalitin knew how to overcome everything: rivals' scientific intrigues, arguments between industrial and military bosses, the mysteries of matter; he had an inner power that broke through all human obstacles. And then the Soviet Union collapsed, an unknown force brought down the previously immutable building of the state, and the production version of Neophyte died under its rubble.

He had never seriously thought about God and had worked fearlessly in his laboratory set up in the defiled chambers of a former monastery; on that one day Kalitin felt what he imagined was God for believers. The dark, impervious strength of matter that resists scientific understanding. That is afraid of titans like Kalitin who had begun a new era in science by learning to look deeper than other scientists into the essence of things—thanks to the merger of the technical capabilities of mass industry and the unlimited power of the planned state economy, which could concentrate previously unheard of resources on the achievement of a scientific goal and give the select scientists not only the means but also the direct, grievous power to achieve it.

Kalitin was experiencing the dull bewilderment of total collapse. He could not take revenge on the destructive power or overcome it. But he so wanted to take revenge on its accomplices, those brainless fools, the cautious bosses, the craven generals with big shoulder boards who could manage nothing more than a cartoon coup attempt, their knees shaking! Or the blind people who wanted something called a free life, stupid people who abandoned their sensible places and labors!

When Kalitin fled soon after, he took this hidden thirst for revenge as his guide. But as years passed it became clear that he had made a shortsighted mistake.

He had rushed.

When the former enemies rejected his knowledge and services, Kalitin could only dream of the restoration of the USSR. There was no life for him outside the laboratory, and a laboratory was possible, he thought, only inside the Soviet Union. He desired that resurrection with a passion greater than that of the million hard-core Communists who rallied in 1993, when the crowd, drunk on the red of hundreds of flags, crushed a policeman to death. He prayed—with the ungainly, doomed prayers of an atheist—to his Neophyte, the unborn divinity of secret weapons, calling on its help if it ever wanted to appear in the world in all its power.

And one day, leafing through a newspaper left by a passenger on the train, Kalitin saw a story on the Chechen war in the Caucasus. He began reading it out of a vengeful curiosity: What problems are those crazy traitors and apostates having?

He had a shaky grasp of his country's geography—he spent decades in his laboratory bubble. So he did not quite understand where these cities and villages were. He was irritated by the alien sounds of Chechnya's place-names and surprised by the weakness of the once-mighty army that could not wipe them off the map. Well, if that army could not defend itself, if its tanks and armored transporters were stopped by an unarmed crowd in the capital, then that army deserved this sort of humiliation, Kalitin thought.

He did not believe the descriptions of the cleansings, torture, and internment centers or filtration camps, of course. Not because he found them morally incomprehensible. He just couldn't believe that any journalist was capable of witnessing or even hearing of them.

A boring trip. The article was in a foreign language, which for him was still riddled with holes of vocabulary and dark corners of grammar. Lazily he skimmed the article, skipping the resisting paragraphs. Suddenly, he was awake. He grew tense and read closely.

The special correspondent apparently had sources among the fighters. Or had been on the wavering front lines. He wrote that a famous field commander had recently been poisoned in his base in a former Pioneer camp. The federal forces had bribed a traitor and had him give the commander some poisoned worry beads, allegedly an ancient and blessed relic. The fighters swore vengeance and called on the world to pay attention to this act of chemical terrorism.

First Kalitin chuckled. A holy relic, poisoned worry beads! What won't they make up next! Pure Shakespeare. The whole story was probably the journalist's invention. Fake news.

But at the same time he remembered his own early experiments with monkeys taken from their breeder. Some of the animals were sent to zoos for the public, and some to Kalitin and his many colleagues. One time at the zoo he looked for a sign of knowledge in the grimacing monkey faces that the sorter had spared them from a terrible fate—an experiment with one of his early formulations that was wonderfully absorbable and took immediate effect, but left a clear trace that he couldn't get rid of.

The animals were given carved wooden objects: spoons, dice, beads, bracelets, alphabet building blocks, pieces of molding, in order to determine how quickly the substance in the wood worked, which types of wood absorbed better, and what shape achieved maximal contact with the skin. Kalitin remembered the wrinkled faces contorted by death. That preparation was accepted and used in production.

Could it be? When he got home, Kalitin read everything he could find about that incident. It all came together. It was his product. An early version he had disdained, but still his child.

The substance was in the right hands. Clearly the special operations group was using it. They must have taken it from the warehouse, as its shelf life, unlike many other products, was unlimited. What if they had reopened the laboratory? Lights burning in the former monastery cells, and someone else sitting at Kalitin's desk?

Belated and useless hope and the sharpest envy tore Kalitin apart.

For years and years with his special chemist's eye he observed the behavior of substances, recognized or not by investigators, substances of different chemical classes and families. They left behind scattered, unexplained deaths that were not connected into a general picture, fatal accidents, established assassinations. They were easy to discern for a connoisseur of death masks of journalists, politicians, and defector agents.

He recognized the substances made by competitors and his own. He felt something new and malevolent—a spree, an orgy—that had not existed in the past. Their time has come at last, Kalitin gloated. Whom could they have stopped in the turmoil of the Soviet Union's collapse in 1991? You can't poison a crowd. You can't strike a blow against something without a center. But now, when there is no solidarity, when there are only separate, isolated figures subconsciously paralyzed by fear . . . the substances were the best choice.

Kalitin knew that his inventions did not simply create specific weapons of death poured into ampoules. He also produced fear. He liked the simple yet paradoxical idea that the best poison is fear. The best poisoning is when people poison themselves. His creations were merely vectors, the sowers of fear. Even the perfect Neophyte. Albeit it was also unique in another of its qualities.

Kalitin painfully regretted not being back on the other side of the border. He knew that they did not forgive people like him. So let them put him in prison, in a secret gulag lab, a *sharashka,* the way they did with scientists in the thirties and forties, let them sentence him to life in prison, if only he could work, work! But then Kalitin would recall the line in the contract he signed: "disclosure is punishable." The sentence awaited him like a bride back home. He had strange, turbulent dreams about execution by firing squad: he experienced it as something intimate that reunited him with his homeland, with his laboratory on a distant island, with his old colleagues, with equipment that remembered his hand; the execution did not kill him, it let him be cleansed, reborn, undid his treason.

But the wakeful daytime Kalitin was skeptical of the nocturnal Kalitin's visions. He thought he knew how to weigh the hurts and the hopes rationally. After all, when he was deciding where to defect, he rejected the stump of Korea created by Stalin, and Communist China, and the states of the Near East.

In part he feared that his homeland had too many eyes and ears there. But more important, he considered himself a man of the first world, not the third. He created methods of killing. But he did not want them used simply because some tribe that had just declared itself a new country hated another tribe. That motive seemed humiliating and unworthy of the scientific truths embodied in his weapons. He had once had a country worth his labors if only because it had enemies of a commensurate scale. That country was gone, so it was better to work for the enemies than for someone in a third, random state on the margins of the original battle.

He had been to the Middle East only once—after the second Iraq campaign. He accompanied a group of inspectors looking for chemical weapons. Kalitin thought that he had already seen and experienced all that: statues pulled down from pedestals, cheering crowds in the streets, corridors of government buildings strewn with documents, bunkers and secret sites abandoned by fleeing guards, test animals dead in their enclosures, microscopes gone blind without electricity, rows of fragile ampoules in soft padded compartments . . .

Now that Kalitin knew his diagnosis, he remembered something else from that trip: the shadow of forgotten and terrible states of antiquity, divine winged bulls and the Hanging Gardens of Babylon, the shadows of innumerable generations turned to silt and dust, to desert sand, so that the names of their rulers would remain in history; the shadow of dams built by pickax and shovel restraining mighty rivers, bearded faces of stone in the halls of ransacked museums, columns and foundations of destroyed temples—the ghosts whispered in a language Kalitin understood, as if he himself were a ghost, the disembodied remains of the past who could understand others who were gone.

Kalitin also understood that even in his country, which was boundlessly generous in death and in honors, human life had never been valued so low and so high; without intervals. It was only there, beyond the edge of the ancient world, that they could help him: to create an entire medical institute if necessary, gather all the luminaries so that he could live, Kalitin, the creator of untraceable death.

When his doctor came in, Kalitin understood just by the look on his face. He was too professionally compassionate. He listened attentively to the doctor's sympathetic, encouraging words, but inside he ran through the names of countries as if they were the names of lifesaving medications the doctor did not know.

He made his decision.

CHAPTER 6

Shershnev enjoyed being involved with the operations. Everything that came before—setting the task, the instructions—was the obligatory prelude to the moment when he opened the file and was left one-on-one with the subject.

First of all, that's what officers in his unit were taught: operations management and extreme action. The *Spetsnaz* skills, the interrogation tactics—that was additional training. During the domestic war their unit was not used for its intended purpose, they were thrown in as reinforcements, and Shershnev was happy to get back to their original tasks, to the familiar style of action.

Some men, Shershnev knew, experienced the pathetic pleasure of peeping schoolboys when they read operative materials. Yes, he admitted, their work, especially surveillance, was in part like voyeurism. He once studied the case of a bohemian artist, womanizer and libertine, who as if to mock them, picked up a new girl every week, took her out to dinner or a movie and then brought her home, and they had to work up a file on each lover, find out who she was and whether she was in their files. By the time the report came back, the artist was sleeping with a new one, and they had to start over. It seemed the colossal operations mechanism was spinning its wheels, the surveillance cars wasted time and gas, the tape recorders captured the same scores of romantic arias, the cameras photographed the same scenes: on the porch of a restaurant, on the street, at the car door. But Shershnev was certain that it was not so. It was their work's irrational redundancy, the ability to randomly expend resources, to the point of ridiculous excess—attempting to keep tabs on every moment and person, as with the libertine artist—that constituted the ritual foundation of their service. Regardless of the result, or whether the agent reports were informative—the surveillance and documentation would continue, because sifting through dust is the manifestation of total power; whoever falls under their purview, their gaze, whoever becomes part of a case becomes significant, exists, is transformed from a nullity, from no one, into the subject.

Shershnev remembered their code names, sometimes written on the cover of a file, sometimes hidden inside.

Stranger. Orpheus. Joker. Wise Guy. Forester. Methodist.

The operative designation: "Treason." "Ideological Diversion."

Lists of agents involved in the case. Lists of accounting incentives. Signatures of colleagues.

The hefty case files. The physical manifestation of the Cheka's special power. The usual ones were two or three volumes. The big ones had eight or ten. The gigantic ones had dozens. Regulations limited their thickness, no more than three hundred pages per volume, so the volumes multiplied, filling the shelves.

The archive repository was the primary venue for their service. Its hidden Hades holding the sealed and sorted sinners. Removing operations files from there gave Shershnev one hundred percent confidence in his own rectitude.

He felt it particularly keenly when he read the file on a former Chechen field commander hiding out in the mountains who had created a legend about himself as born fighter for independence. Yet not so long ago, he had been chairman of a kolkhoz and had been part of a case they were working on: speculation, selling off part of the harvest, illegal acquisition of hard currency. They had reports on this from their agent on the kolkhoz board. Utterances against the state. His brother was arrested for embezzlement. His father died in exile in Kazakhstan.

The operations case was started when Shershnev was still in school, only dreaming of joining the service. That fact was additional confirmation of the right Shershnev had to take over the case. The actual materials in the file, collected by other officers who might be retired by now, formatted, entered, and numbered, predetermined their interactions with the subject. Attentive Shershnev found an unnoticed hook that allowed them to recruit the man who would hand over the worry beads; just one inconspicuous line in an old agent's report turned into a successful operation.

That's why Shershnev liked working with operations files. But he had never seen anything like this before.

Twenty-four volumes. A personal record for him.

They did not give him the actual volumes. Only some rather unconnected copied excerpts. Essentially, Shershnev had only the beginning and the end of an enormous file. He knew he would not have been given even that much, but he had to be able to identify the subject with total certainty, even his appearance had changed many times; computer reconstructions of possible features did not guarantee one hundred percent recognition.

When they told him that an undercover chemist was the subject this time, he assumed that the documents would have gaps, redacted names of special products and special factories. Shershnev always considered these internal secrecy measures necessary and sometimes pointed out any lapses to the archivists.

But here Shershnev felt a vague whiff of anxiety for the first time. They had not given him enough time to prepare, to familiarize himself with the situation on location and they were rushing him.

The expurgated file added to uncertainty: Would everything be taken into account, would things go as needed?

Shershnev understood that this was his big moment, delayed by his previous success. He had no doubts about the right of his bosses to give the order, its fairness, or his readiness to carry it out.

But deep in a far corner of his mind lay the wish that the order had been given to someone else. It was the quiet voice of professional superstition. It was all too much of a coincidence the way that old operation and this new order dovetailed.

There wasn't a single word in the file that said what the chemist heading a secret laboratory had worked on. But Shershnev, naturally, guessed where the substance they used on the worry beads had originated. For the first time in his career, he felt a strange, superfluous closeness to the subject.

Shershnev rubbed his temples. Yesterday came up in his memory. The mock execution of his son. The return trip, Maxim's silence. The jokes and laughter of his friends. The Pioneer camp, a twin of the one left in the foothills of the Caucasus. The long line of trucks carrying shipping containers that crossed the intersection while they waited.

It's all nonsense, he told himself. The worries, false fears, imaginary signs at the start of a truly important case. Just don't notice them. Endure them. Pull yourself together. He would talk to Maxim when he got back. There was no time now. Shershnev did not like putting things off like this until he got back; he usually felt that no loose threads should be hanging, but now he changed his own rule.

He breathed in and held it. He waited thirty seconds. Blinked hard. And opened the file again. Well, he'd work with what they had. He would try to look into the abyss, into emptiness.

Shershnev never believed that you could learn anything about a person from his childhood and adolescence. Take that field commander, who had been born in a mud hut on the steppe, who had returned with his pardoned people from Kazakhstan, where they were sent by Stalin, to the Chechen mountains that he had never seen, graduated from college and was elected chairman of a kolkhoz—could he have ever imagined on the eve of 1991 that he would be a commander in a few years, or how many soldiers would be in his unit, or how his life would intersect with Shershnev's?

Now however, with only the beginning and end of another man's life, Shershnev felt a new kind of thrill.

Shershnev undid the binding and moved the photograph submitted by the applicant closer to the light.

CHAPTER 7

Kalitin didn't take a single photograph from his old life into his new one. He was allegedly going on a four-day business trip. He packed accordingly, in case they checked at customs. Four shirts, trousers, coat, a pair of shoes: the obvious necessities. He hid money in the suitcase lining. Neophyte went into his carry-on: concealed in what appeared to be a bottle of men's toilet water, popular at the time.

Later Kalitin realized he could have brought photographs, his furniture, a box of secret documents. His brand-new foreign passport had been marked in the border control system. The lazy customs agents didn't even look at his luggage.

Just a few years earlier, Kalitin would not have been allowed abroad. They would not have given him a passport. Had he requested one, they would have considered him mad, removed him from his job, turned him in, and started an investigation. Not just that—in those days, even his distant relatives were denied foreign travel, even when the travel had credible explanations.

Now the state's muscles were relaxed, like those of a dead dog used in Kalitin's experiments. The defector walked unnoticed through the open jaws. Actually, it was but a brief moment of weakness; the jaws soon clamped shut again.

The clothes he brought were what he wore for special occasions: Party bureau meetings, a delegation of high officials on an inspection visit. The trousers were too narrow, the jacket sleeves too long, the shirts too tight. Kalitin had bought them himself, after his wife's death. His wife saw him intuitively, she did not make mistakes in size or style. But he seemed unable to even take the measure of his own body, he did not have a simple visual sense, the secret sign of harmony with the world of things.

The first days. A foreign life. Foreign, like another man's clothes. Constant fear that they would turn him in, send him back. Take him to the embassy. But one morning he got up and at first did not realize that his shirt fit; he had lost weight. That day they informed him that he would receive refuge.

Kalitin kept that lucky shirt, white with light blue patterns. He threw out everything else, bought a new wardrobe, going to a store without guards for the first time. The container of Neophyte spent months in a hiding place he had created before turning himself over to counterintelligence.

Now the container was in his home safe. The opaque bottle of men's toilet water, long out of fashion and no longer produced, an eccentricity of a gentleman averse to change in his habits.

Kalitin took that shirt with him to the hospital for his checkup. When he was released, he put it on, a talisman from the past.

He looked at himself several times in the rearview mirror, trying to find signs of malevolent changes, wanting to compare his faces in the long enfilade of time. But he had only his present self for comparison. The old photographs were in his abandoned apartment. The investigators would have confiscated them and added them to his file.

He didn't take any new photographs. He tried to avoid being photographed, even in random tourist shots. Looked out for the omnivorous cars taking panoramic street photos for Google Maps. The video cameras in airports and train stations. That was the recommendation they made, since his doctors did not want him to have plastic surgery. Kalitin found an attenuated but precious pleasure in obedience, which he had felt more vividly in his former life when he filled out secret forms in accordance with instructions.

Now he regretted not having photos from the past, it was as if the record of his activity had not been saved in a computer game and he was left unable to recall his own image. There were no subjects that had known him before. Kalitin thought about his old home, now covered with a patina of estrangement in his memory. The fingerprint men must have tested all the smooth surfaces, taken the impressions, since the investigators did not know for sure whether he had run away, or vanished, or had been kidnapped. And then what? What happened to the furniture? Did they take it away, throw it out? The couch, the stupid foldout couch with creaking springs where Vera conceived their unborn child . . . Kalitin felt the news of imminent demise squashing, chewing through all lines of defense, gradually turning his thoughts toward possible death.

Home, he had to get home. Hide behind the solid walls. Rest. Gather strength. There was one more flight ahead.

The turnoff from the highway. The road led to a wide valley. The city outskirts began. A garden center with a display of plants;

chubby, red-cheeked gnomes in caps; and stout faceless nymphs, covered in road dust. Supermarket. Park.

The central high street. Trolley coming from the train station. Cafe, kebab house. On the right, the cathedral, a large cathedral for a small city that had grown rich on the salt deposits in surrounding mountains, a city that worshipped salt but did not forget the church. The deposits were exhausted and abandoned: the last of the salt had been eaten with soup by the Kaiser's soldiers. A miner's body turned to stone was exhibited in the regional museum—put to work for the city even after his death, bringing in entrance fees. A small steam train drove children through a nearby tunnel; during the war, the locals used it as a bomb shelter, for the train station here was an important junction.

The city was coming to an end. The road headed up the valley slope. Here he knew who owned the fields, whose cows were grazing on the slope, whose horses were in the paddock.

Ruins of a water mill, a restaurant that serves roast pork and baked trout. The bright tiles of new roofs on village houses, floating in saccharine flower gardens. Smooth turn along a low cliff. A church on the stone ledge carved by a glacier that crept down into the valley a thousand years ago. The ancient church rejecting the confectionary luxury of the city cathedral, compressed by heavy, disproportional buttresses, which had collapsed and been rebuilt, retaining traces of various layers of brickwork. Below were enormous round boulders, clumsily worked stones, then neat rectangular blocks, and above them dark, almost soot-black, brick. The roof made of flat shale slabs was covered with moss. The cross tilted to one side. The carved stained-glass sun over the main entrance had dimmed. Beyond the fence—the cemetery arborvitae, the sagging headstones of salt magnates, rusted crosses. Even neglected and desolate, the church still amazed Kalitin with its grim, sleeping power; sometimes he compared himself to it and thought that their proximity was no accident.

Kalitin looked back at the road, just in time. Around the bend, hidden by the cliff, Pastor Travniček was slowly crossing the road.

He had arrived in these parts about six years before Kalitin. They said that Travniček had served in big cities, was considered on track to become a bishop. But suddenly he ended up here, in a forsaken corner, on an ancient mountain border, near a city with exhausted salt deposits, in a village where the old were dying and the young—those who had not moved to greener pastures—rarely went to church.

Kalitin knew what had happened. He liked the knowledge, because it confirmed that the church was merely an institution, and a very earthly one at that.

Travniček was a monster. He had suffered a rare skin disease, perhaps caught a virus, which was the eternal risk of working in densely populated areas, amid microparticles of other people's skin, other people's breath—and his face had turned to stone, a bumpy, lichen mask.

They exiled the monster, thought Kalitin, so he would not scare parishioners, not ruin the solemn ritual with his face so like a humanized lizard, his snakelike gaze beneath scaly lids.

Even now, with one foot in the grave, Kalitin still felt a fastidious gratitude that the pastor had taken on the horrible but singular misery that could have stricken any other person.

Hearing the car, Travniček turned. The pastor always turned, bringing his face in the other's field of vision so tactfully that Kalitin was revolted by his humility. Kalitin, despite himself, despite his scorn for faith, felt in Travniček a power similar to the one slumbering in the church where he served. He wondered what this man, capable of living placidly with a troll's face, was doing as a priest, among all these pious nonentities?

The pastor tried to wave down Kalitin. Kalitin opened his hands to show he couldn't stop; it was rude, but he was in a hurry and someone else would give the pastor a ride. Then Kalitin remembered that Travniček had a car, not a big truck but a new compact SUV. Maybe it was broken? Kalitin considered backing up but the road was already going downhill before flying up the hill, where he would see the church in the rearview mirror for the last time, and then he would be on the dusty, unpaved road, apple trees, hills, hunter's huts on the slopes . . . Home.

Refuge.

It was only then that he realized how desperately he wanted to be there.

Kalitin was proud that he had guessed right away, had sensed the essence of his future sanctuary immediately.

They had suggested he move to a rural area, where all the residents knew one another and would easily notice an outsider. Kalitin, used to a closed city, reluctantly looked at a few places. There weren't many offers. People rarely changed their homes and fates in such areas. All the houses for sale were old farmhouses intended for large, no longer present families. They were crowded too close to neighbors. There was something pathetic and bewildering about them. It seemed to him that the houses themselves and not the bankrupt owners had suffered a life-changing collapse, and the connectivity of things had vanished from nails, cement, and spackling.

Kalitin was ready to go back. But in the last town, the real estate agent, a thin and severe man of seventy or so, listened to his evasive explanation, intentionally ungrammatical, about wanting peace and quiet to finish his research, and then started his long green Mercedes, the size of a hearse, saying he had a suitable house.

Kalitin was surprised that the agent must have understood more about him than he had wanted to reveal. In the vulnerable moment of moving, in the moment of a forced choice limited by time and cash, a person will show a little of his true self. Given his profession—finding houses, transforming clients' secret wishes into walls and roofs, locating protection from displaced fears and hidden phobias, from a dangerous past—the real estate agent guessed what Kalitin was and what he needed as a defector.

The agent died seven years ago. Kalitin had attended his funeral. The family thought it was a neighborly gesture. Kalitin had been accepted in the village, he fit in among these insular people who disliked strangers, because he was like that himself. Seeing him there, Pastor Travniček nodded his stone-like head in approval and benevolence. But Kalitin, he had come to bury a witness.

He was certain that the real estate agent had not left behind any personal notes, any diary nonsense. Only receipts, accounts, contracts, disciplined and uncommunicative. The pastor gave a short sermon, something about the gift of honesty. Kalitin liked looking at the shellacked coffin lid, beneath a spattering of infrequent but large raindrops, like the ones that fell on the first day he came here.

They had driven in silence. They passed the church, the village, the yellowed slopes billowing like sails, the dells overgrown with hazel and echoing with the sound of bells.

The road, surrounded by apple trees, led upward. Boars ran out of the bushes, feasting on fallen apples. The entire valley was visible—without a single house. The eye could not find a place where it could be hidden: no clumps of trees, no hollows. It seemed the agent was driving for nothing. Kalitin would have stopped and turned around: they had passed some invisible line that marked the limit of inhabited places and entered into unpopulated territory.

The road smoothly bent to the left, clearing away the optical illusion of the landscape that hid the upper level of the valley. There, in the shadow of a beech forest that grew along the ridges of the hills, stood a solitary house.

The house was wooden. But the wood seemed to have ossified, the way the supports do in salt mines. A house composed of dark logs, as if the bitter, cool juices of this stony land still slept in the dry felled trunks. Blinds in the windows. A few apple trees higher up the slope, gone wild, losing variety and species. The nearby mouth of the forest where the road ended, sending the scents of the brook's flinty coolness and the sweet rot of the broad, slow-dying beech leaves.

Unexpectedly a blue-gray cloud rose heavily from behind a hill. Large drops, soft and lisping somehow, began to fall. The agent opened an umbrella, but Kalitin was already striding toward the house, feeling those insouciant drops falling from a nearby cloud.

Kalitin expected furniture inside. For some reason he envisioned a grand piano, strangers' photos over the wardrobe, red-and-white checked tablecloths, stag horns above the fireplace, a worn leather couch. The house was completely empty. Just a pile of ash and coals in the fireplace, as if the previous residents had taken away everything changeable, which could pass from hand to hand and switch owners, and had burned everything important, essential.

At first he was discouraged, upset, as if the ashes truly were the remains of someone's life. But then, accustomed to semiofficial housing, he felt the strange charm of the emptiness that he would have to fill with new things that were his and his alone. He felt the twilight allure of the forest. The quiet call of the hills, their readiness to stand guard, shield, be vigilant in the night.

It was at that moment that he decided to buy the house. The real estate agent carefully propped his damp umbrella against the wall and spoke slowly, ceremoniously.

"I think you will like it here. It is a good place."

CHAPTER 8

Shershnev was in the first row of economy. Next to him, in 6C, was Major Grebenyuk. His partner. They had been offered business class, but Shershnev refused: no need to be so visible.

The lieutenant colonel looked at his boarding pass once again: ALEXANDER IVANOV, 6D. He had a passport and visa in that name. Although they were brought through a special corridor bypassing customs control and inspection, a border officer still stamped the passport.

The crew—it was a state airline—had been alerted there were special passengers on board. His partner, a military technician, an engineer with epaulets, had a bottle of deodorant from an expensive toiletries line in his carry-on that complied with airline requirements: under three ounces or one hundred milliliters. The specialists chose the brand, deciding which bottle was more convenient to accurately reproduce. They had considered sending the substance by diplomatic pouch and picking it up on the other side of the border, but they decided that bringing it along was faster and safer, since they would not have to meet up with the embassy courier, who could be tailed.

They flew at night. A late flight that would land early in

the morning, when the sleepy, tired border guards and customs agents would be less picky. His partner was settling down to sleep. He leaned back his seat, even though that was not allowed during takeoff. The cabin purser did not reprimand him—she knew who they were.

The plane was still at the gate. They were waiting for some idiots in business class. Probably blotto, thought Shershnev. Afraid of flying, so they drank for courage.

He wouldn't have refused a shot himself. He felt uncomfortable. Behind them was a foreign couple—Czechs, he thought—with two children. The infant, despite his concern, fell asleep quickly. But the girl seated behind Shershnev, an active, skinny kid with thin blond braids, whom he had noted at check-in, when she tried to jump onto the baggage conveyor belt, kept kicking his seat.

The blows hurt his lower back. It was economy class; the upholstery was pathetic. Shershnev regretted not taking business class. He had turned around once already, glaring at her. She seemed to quiet down. But a minute later, she was kicking his seat again, harder, more persistently.

They were under orders to keep a low profile on the plane. No changing places with other passengers. No getting into arguments. The girl must have sensed it and mocked Shershnev. He spoke to the parents in English and in Russian. They either did not understand or because they could not control the child pretended not to understand. He made gestures to show that their daughter was disturbing him, but the mother merely smiled and shrugged.

Passengers bored by the wait were looking at them from neighboring rows. Shershnev thought it better to get back in his seat and not call the stewardess. Everything the state had provided him with was useless against a little brat who took him for a weakling who could not fight back.

He even thought about the bottle in his partner's carry-on bag. How he could get it out and . . .

Suddenly he imagined that the girl was sensing his hidden thoughts. In the ether. She sensed Shershnev, not Ivanov. The real Shershnev. Unusual, nervous children can do that. He knew. When Shershnev returned from his second tour in the Chechen war, Maxim, an infant, cried hysterically whenever he picked him up. He grew rigid, lost his breath, screamed until he was hoarse—and calmed down easily in Marina's arms. A few weeks later, Shershnev felt that he was getting over his wartime experiences—and his son allowed his father to hold him.

The girl could see right through him. And she was protecting herself as best she could.

Shershnev turned and peered into the space between seats. The girl looked back at him: with incomprehension and anxious curiosity. Shershnev wanted to crush her with his stare. But then he remembered a game he used to play with Maxim long ago. He got his pen and drew a funny face on the fleshy pillow between thumb and forefinger, bending his fingers to make it look like the little person wanted to talk.

The girl smiled and relaxed, she fell asleep before his eyes, as if she had just needed a small dose of fun to relieve her tension. Shershnev wiped off the ink and also relaxed. The late passengers finally arrived, and the plane pulled back from the gate. The crew started the safety instructions, a cork popped softly in business class and champagne fizzed.

Shershnev liked being in the sky, in a plane. His thoughts were especially clear in flight. Naturally, the lieutenant colonel could not bring along even a line of documentation about the subject. He was a completely different person now, the businessman Ivanov, traveling with his friend to drink beer and eat sausages, pick up pretty girls, buy gifts. But Shershnev had memorized the most important things, and now he intended to think things through and pull it all together. He didn't have to do it, analysis was not required of him. However, the subject was no longer an abstract, theoretical target, as he should have been, but a phantom, a shadow looming in the distance. He had taken on a strange, illusory freedom of behavior, and Shershnev wanted to subordinate him again, reassert his own power over him, the power that Shershnev had had over the doomed field commander.

But his mind wandered, as if the subject tried to defend himself from being understood and enslaved, tried to slip away. Then Shershnev started thinking about another person capable—that was the operative system in finding approaches to the subject—of leading him to the right conclusions.

Igor Yuryevich Zakharyevsky. He died as an academician, lieutenant general in the medical service. Laureate and so on. Zakharyevsky was too significant to be hidden entirely, so he had a public, overt identity.

An academician. Distant relative. Luminary.

Naturally his emblem, the bowl and snake, was a cover. He didn't do medicine. What he did do Shershnev was not supposed to know. But no one could stop him from guessing.

Zakharyevsky. He remembered that name.

When Shershnev began working, there was almost no one left in the ranks with prewar experience. Those who had served during the period of "violations of socialist legality," as they called it in the political training classes. The father of one of Shershnev's colleagues was a retired colonel, in scientific counterintelligence.

Winter. Yes, winter. A departmental house of light brick in the middle of Moscow. A birthday party. Cognac sent for the guest of honor from somewhere in the Caucasus; his old colleagues supplied the gift. Smoking breaks in the kitchen. Their youthful drunken argument about what "one of us" meant and can you recognize a future traitor by intuition, by sixth sense.

The retired officer listened in silence. Then he chopped his hand through the air, as if chopping off someone's head. With unexpected force, seemingly trying to convince himself as well as them, he told them about Zakharyevsky. Zakharyevsky's cousin, also a scientist and specialist in cattle breeding, had been accused of falsifying results of experiments in order to sabotage the upturn in agriculture. He was executed on the sentence handed down by a troika, a military tribunal, in 1937. And rehabilitated in 1959.

"Zakharyevsky, however," he said firmly, albeit with a heavy asthmatic wheeze, "became an academician. Even though he could have nursed a deep anger against the Soviet regime because of his cousin. But he understood that a mistake had been made. The Party trusted him. And he merited that trust. One of us," the former counterintelligence agent summarized, stretching out the word "us," to confirm his commonality with Zakharyevsky and declare publicly the state's and service's claim upon the academician, in which he played a small personal part.

Now things came together for Shershnev. Zakharyevsky. So he must have used his position to help his cousin's relatives get work in a closed city. Work they should not have been given: it didn't matter that the executed zoologist had been rehabilitated later, children of enemies were trusted very selectively. Thanks to Zakharyevsky, they cunningly gained access to the storehouse of secrets, where everything was special, even the police and prosecutors. No surprise that the subject had become his student and successor.

At the briefing they told Shershnev there was a great probability that the subject wanted to return to the homeland. He was unconsciously waiting to be punished and was unlikely to resist. On the contrary, he would accept vengeance as his due.

But his guess about Zakharyevsky's cunning, having accepted the loss of his cousin—and had he?—while managing to obtain cover for relatives, told Shershnev: no. The subject would not surrender just like that. He would try to save himself—at any cost.

Strangely, that pleased Shershnev.

CHAPTER 9

Kalitin shut the door behind him, turned on the entry light, and glanced around at the corners. He had lived alone for too long, he had almost no interaction with others, and he was interested solely in himself. Deprived of research, of real work, he scrupulously observed his own habits, registered the preferences or antipathies that explained them, mere stubs, wax casts of the bigger emotions that had once ruled him.

Even now, as he brought into his house the terrible news of the disease that would relentlessly destroy his daily rituals, acquired over years, take him away from his desk, chair, and book shelves, whose existence would outlast his and were no longer absolutely in his possession—Kalitin had to check the corners: Were there any rats?

As a child, he was not afraid of animals that usually scare children, dogs for example; the closed city was too new, it arose in the idyll of the woods, people moved there hurriedly without knowing what to expect and left their pets with relatives. There were no stray dogs, because there was nowhere from which they might come.

As an adolescent, he did not seek pleasure in torturing

creatures. Later, during his studies and work, he treated animals indifferently. An entire host of them, thousands of mice, hundreds of dogs, rabbits, monkeys, dozens of horses, goats, and sheep died in torment—but that had been necessary, they served a greater good. If he could have managed without test subjects, he would not have used them. But nature did not want to give up its secrets without force, without sacrificial death, without dull foam in the mouth.

When tests were performed on dummies, he did not see the process and only read the results. Age. Weight. Disease. Reaction to the substance. The dummies excited him intensely—he wanted to delve deeper into the mystery of human death. Kalitin saw that there were no two identical deaths. Similar complexion, identical age, but the final moments passed in different ways, the symptoms of the final agony were expressed in different ways. Physiology? Psychology? Character? Fate? He did not perceive the test dummies as people. They were an infinitely complex collection of parameters, animated brainteasers. He did not need explanations that these were state criminals sentenced to death, corpses in waiting. Those legalistic details stayed outside the testing chamber. Inside, there was only the body and the substance in it, injected by the lab technician skilled at assuaging any sense of deceit, pretending to be a kindly doctor.

Of all living creatures that had been in his power, populating the laboratory ark, Kalitin prioritized only the rats.

On the Island, in the ancient monastery building, they had hundreds of artificially bred rats, identical, docile fools. But from somewhere in the monastery cellars, deep down in the limestone, abandoned, sealed off, in the auxiliary and working rooms of the laboratory, which only the most select, tested, and retested personnel could enter, real, feral rats came and went unhindered.

The first to be defeated were the construction laborers, armed with cement, plaster, iron, brick, and ground glass. There were only a few with the level of security clearance required to work in the lab. They worked assiduously to fill and seal all the holes they found. But the rats kept coming from somewhere, devouring sandwiches left in briefcases, ruining paper and cardboard. The old-timers said you couldn't get rid of the rats because they swam over from the numerous grain barges that traveled the river. But the rats continued their outrageous behavior in the winter, when the river iced over and the barges had to wait in backwaters.

Then they sent a rat catcher with an express security clearance; they had all kinds of specialists in their system! The rat catcher with all his powders didn't succeed, either.

That's when Kalitin announced the competition, as if for fun. He was affronted that some pathetic rodents had the run of his place while they, the poison masters, the researchers and creators of the most toxic substances in the world, could not destroy them.

It turned out that everyone was sick of the rats. His staff, especially the young people, were zealous in developing recipes and inventing traps. It seemed the end had come for the rats, and Kalitin joked: see what science can do! But he soon discovered that not all of the rats were dying. They destroyed most of them, but some, at the cost of their companions' deaths, learned to recognize bait and avoid traps. There weren't many of them, just a few. But they couldn't kill them, and all human tricks had limited effect.

Kalitin learned their traces and habits. He could tell which rat had visited. One, a huge rat with a bitten tail, seemed to tease him, flashing by in the dim corridor and then vanishing. Kalitin could have gotten rid of them, but only by poisoning everything, endangering himself and the staff, paying a price that was not worth a rat's life.

Ever since, he had had a watchful, uneasy respect for rats, as if nature was showing him an important exception that had to be taken into account. Later, in his new life, when he felt like a cornered rat, Kalitin discovered to his surprise that this association reassured him, as if he had become that exception to the laws of hunt and capture, manifested in only one breed of creatures.

He received a sign that his sensations were correct. A sign that came from the long bygone past of his new house. With an unpredictable rhyme it merged the two halves of his biography, separated by defection, border, death sentence.

Cars never came to his house, except for the yellow postal van and the taxis he ordered. It was on a dead-end road. No landmarks nearby, so tourists wouldn't wander in by mistake. Hunting was banned, leaving the boar population to expand, but the old hunting towers still stood on the slopes and along the brook.

However eleven, yes, eleven years ago he saw a car beneath his windows, a shabby gray sedan, an unobtrusive vehicle used for surveillance and hired killers. Even though Kalitin realized that people sent to kill him would not reveal themselves that openly, he quickly went down to the cellar, trying not to be visible through the windows, opened the gun cupboard, and returned upstairs with a loaded rifle.

The doorbell rang; long, demanding: in the manner of the police or courier delivery. Kalitin decided not to open the door, even though his own car parked under the overhang showed that he was probably in. He was afraid to approach the peephole. And he was afraid, completely irrationally, that if this were say an insurance agent, or surveyor, or an official from the nature preserve—they would spread talk that the professor did not open the door even though he was home and someone, a someone he made up in his own head, would suspect that the inhabitant of the lonely house on the hill had something to fear and something to hide.

He had not yet equipped the house with the soundproof steel door, made to look like wood. The surveillance cameras that he could monitor from the computer. Kalitin could not see who was at the door without giving away his presence.

The visitor stepped down from the porch and started walking around the house. Through a space between the curtains, Kalitin saw a face—a typical Englishman, curly reddish hair, glasses, the only Englishman for dozens of kilometers around—certainly not sent by the homeland, they sent their own people, Slavs—and it wasn't a visitor from his new masters, they would have warned him. A journalist? Had he sniffed something out? A leak? Someone turned him in?

Kalitin realized that fear had made him forget his secret companion, the joker, Neophyte. The preparation slept in its reliable flask behind the door of a special safe for active substances. Kalitin suddenly imagined what could happen if Neophyte woke on its own and found even a micron-sized opening in the hermetic flask, got free, bypassing the dosimeter, and escaped completely, dissolving instantaneously in the air. He would fall asleep without knowing that he was dead. The curious Englishman would be dead. The swallows that made a nest under the eaves and their babies. Butterflies and mosquitoes. Tree beetles, worms, woodlice, even moles. In the morning the mailman would see a corpse by the house, he would call the police, they would break down the door but find and smell nothing except the heavy, particular smell of yesterday's death. Neophyte would be gone, lost amid the atoms and molecules of the astral plane. Only an experienced and sensitive senior officer, an old bloodhound, would say, sniffing in irritated surprise, "A luxurious house, and clean, but it smells of bedbugs!"

His deputies would assure him that it did not smell of bedbugs.

Kalitin chuckled. He had such a clear vision of the dead Englishman, so incongruous and comic in his plaid wool jacket among the fresh molehills, that he stopped being afraid of him. It was as if Neophyte had sighed in its sleep, and that breath was enough to chase always the fears of its imperfect creator.

Kalitin hid the rifle in the closet. Open? Not open? If it's a journalist, it's better to find out what he knows. Better to have a chance to give his own version.

Deceive.

Justify.

He opened the door.

The Englishman turned toward the sound. A thin ocher sweater under his jacket. Light classic jeans. Suede moccasins. Camera on a strap over his shoulder. A big, expensive camera, clearly often used, since some paint had worn off the lens rim. Thin. Not an athlete, but agile and energetic. Externally a polite friendliness, embarrassment at disturbing the owner. Inside, a masterful self-confidence, a trained ability to play along with whatever the owner said and in five or six phrases bring the conversation to the point. A journalist. Excited, following a trail, and for all that, like a loud shot missing the mark, missing Kalitin's particular destiny.

He wasn't there for him, but for some other mission that was inciting him, prodding, filling him with the joy of discovery. The Englishman was staring with the sharp, visionary greed of an archaeologist, the madman Schliemann—but at the house, not the owner.

Kalitin knew who the previous owners were: descendants of salt traders. The house had been their country villa. Allegedly one member of the family made a career under the Nazis in occupied Poland, and Kalitin assumed the journalist was writing a book and had come to learn about that official of the general governorship. Unexpectedly, Kalitin realized this made him uncomfortable; as if he were tied to the former owners by the shackles of inherited family secrets, and the obnoxious visitor was trying to learn about his life, too.

He would have kept it to a quick chat on the porch. But he did not want the journalist to notice his taciturn reluctance to talk and keep it in his professionally long and tenacious memory, so he played the part of a friendly and bored simpleton and invited him in.

If only the journalist could have known that there were two related stories associated with the house, that the shell had landed a second time in the same crater, he would have noticed how unexpectedly deep and animated was the new owner's surprise when he was told why the journalist was there.

Beyond the nearby mountains, divided by an angry, restless river, beyond the dark crests covered in old forests that had borrowed the long life of stone, there was a fortress that had known prisoners of several centuries and realms. During the war, it had been a concentration camp.

In spring of 1945 the roar of war had quieted over the eastern plains, the artillery fire had dimmed. That was when they came to the house—along the old grass-covered road across the mountains, along the path of woodcutters who made the supports for the salt mines, where neither motorcycle nor car could travel. Several SS officers serving as guards and a scientist who experimented on the camp prisoners. One of the SS knew about this remote villa. He had been a guest there.

Germany had lost the war. Below, in the valleys, in larger towns Allies set up garrisons. But here, closer to the peaks, in the mountain forests and meadows, there was no regime yet. The former owners had already abandoned the villa property and fled. The accidental residents could relax there.

In fact, the journalist was trying to find out if this was the house. Turned out it was. He had a description given during interrogation by an officer of the camp guards, arrested in the British occupation zone. The rest had vanished, gone along the ratlines, the secret escape routes from Europe across the ocean to the other continent.

He said ratlines, in his flawless English. And then with his student intonation he repeated it in German: *Rattenlinien*.

"Escaping rats always use the same paths," the journalist had said then.

He meant the underground network of secret aid for fugitives: officials who would issue false documents and trusted people like priests and policemen; seamen who would take illegal passengers. He was writing a book about medics in camps, and it was easy to talk to Kalitin, an émigré from the land of the victors. He was enthralled by his hunt for ghosts of the past and therefore blind in the present. He asked permission to photograph the house and look at all of it. He peeked into the cellar, passing within a yard of Neophyte in the safe. He asked about the old furniture. No, nothing was left, Kalitin told him sincerely.

When the journalist had taken his leave, Kalitin instantly took a heart pill.

It was not just the ratlines that had amazed him.

In his previous life he had known only one German scientist who had worked in a concentration camp. He had been brought back as a trophy after the war by Uncle Igor, Igor Yuryevich Zakharyevsky.

Officially, the German did not exist. The closed city was his prison. But he was a sinister specialist, who had performed experiments that even they would not have countenanced; he had looked much farther beyond the edge of pain and death—and he was ready to share his experience scrupulously.

Kalitin remembered how Zakharyevsky told him the prisoner's story. Kalitin was outraged, even though he had already taken more than one life. But that German, he might have tortured and killed our soldiers; perhaps Kalitin's maternal grandfather, a mathematician who fought in the artillery and died in a POW camp, had fallen into his hands.

Kalitin was ready to kill the German. But a few days later, he noticed that his anger had waned. He still hated the prisoner scientist, he thought, but he was ready to work with him.

First of all, Zakharyevsky wanted that to happen: his plan was to develop a substance based on the previous generation elaborated by the German. Second, Kalitin appreciated the prisoner's verified scientific method. And third, he felt, despite his upbringing, despite the compulsory image of the enemy he was taught, that there was a strange, forbidden affinity in their inner desires, that went deeper than nationality, ideology, enmity: to find the shortest path to knowledge that makes one an indispensable creator regardless of the circumstances. This gives the greatest protection and power. The German proved by his own example that it was possible.

Guessing his new colleague's feelings, the German did not push himself forward, did not force himself on him, did not talk about the past. He just worked: steadily and swiftly. Eventually Kalitin realized that this lonely old man was closer to him than the general and Party bosses who ran the laboratory. They were his own people by blood and citizenship, but alien by their nature, while the German was alien, as much as one could be, and yet his own. One of the people who hid from the state within the state, making it serve him and paying with loyal service, merging with it to the point where you could not tell who directed whom.

It was that German who, once he understood that his junior colleague was ready for the next, even more difficult level of knowledge, opened his eyes to the shadow within the shadow: the dual past of the laboratory, that is, of the place, the Island, where it was located. The German had been there before—before the war, before Hitler was chancellor, when a secret joint Soviet-German testing ground was located there.

Even though he knew some of the dark secrets of the Island, Kalitin refused to believe this. Then the German described the installation from memory—the location of the airfield, the wooden laboratory building, staff barracks, the menagerie, the guardhouse, the fence line; he told him where in the present-day, enlarged testing ground you could find old foxholes and craters left by artillery fire; he took Kalitin there, dug around with a stick in the dried grass, showed him a shell casing left after an explosion. It had German markings. Seeing that Kalitin still had doubts, the German took him to the archives; there was a special section for documents brought out from various European countries after the war, heaps of papers from various scientific institutes, some charred, warped by water. No one had gone through them carefully; Klaus opened a nondescript army box for Kalitin. It held reports on joint experiments. In 1933, German scientists took them to Germany. In 1945 a special NKVD team found them in the ruins and brought them back.

Kalitin read, recognizing the locations described, the names of scientists from the Soviet side. Zakharyevsky's name appeared. Kalitin knew it all: the specifics of the climate that appeared in the course of the experiments, the scientific logic.

And there was Klaus's last name.

He sensed that he no longer consider Klaus an enemy.

Having said goodbye to the journalist, Kalitin started thinking about Klaus. The knowledge he had revealed. Kalitin pondered the systematic tautologies of history, elicited by the extreme rareness of truly secret places, good for hiding, for protecting a secret. He thought about himself and how he had chosen a house on someone's old path. A ratline. That meant he could count on its patronage, on the enduring luck of refugees, since the people who had been protecting him now wanted to kill him.

The journalist had shown him copies of the interrogation pages. The guard officer who had a technical education gave evidence about the experiments in the camp. There was much he did not know, he mixed up terminology, but Kalitin instantly understood: it was the work of a butcher. Cheap, crude death for masses herded to slaughter. Visible, obvious death that did not hide itself. They must have taken the documentation with them or hidden it somewhere along the way—like a bank deposit, like stocks that had temporarily lost value but could have their former prices restored if the new masters of Europe, hiding their mutual hostility, should need to kill someone: Communists, for example. Or the capitalist bourgeoisie.

Kalitin had left a secret cache like that in his homeland, a tube buried beneath an inconspicuous tree in the woods. It was like looking into an ideal, absolute mirror, and he looked without surprise, without anxiety, as if he had lived all those disjointed lives, separated by time. Or at least was the link connecting them.

Ever since that meeting, Kalitin imagined there might be a rat in the house. He lived cleanly, far from the village, why would rats come there—and yet he kept imagining a gray shadow.

He took off his coat and lit the fire. Twilight was falling rapidly. Darkness came quickly in the valley, as if the hills, trees, and grasses radiated it. He looked out the window. A plane flew above the dimmed and darkened clouds. Its feathery trail was still reddish yellow in the light. Splitting wood the old way for kindling,

Kalitin thought about the plane and the people in it. Where was it going, was the captain competent, how old was the plane?

Kalitin was ready to think about anything at all, do whatever, split kindling, haul firewood—anything to put off the moment when he would be home for good, and the thought of death would return with new, almost overwhelming force; it would go on the attack.

He knew he was in for a sleepless night. A long night of fear and memory. He wanted flames in the fireplace, the humming updraft in the chimney, and the sweet smoke of apple logs, so hard they made a ringing sound, unyielding to fire.

CHAPTER 10

Standing in line at passport control, Shershnev felt neither anger nor impatience, even though things were dragging out; forty minutes wasted. When he started an assignment, he always thought he had tons of time. No matter the delays, whatever the obstacles, he would still be a step or two ahead of the subject.

They had chosen an entry point in a country that did not have its own strong counterintelligence. He and his partner were to go through control with the second dozen passengers from their flight: the first dozen received the most attention.

But first they had to change the broken boarding stairs. Then the bus circled the airport for a long time. When they were released into the arrivals hall, there were hundreds of passengers from flights that had arrived after them.

The border guards were in no hurry. There were only two counters for non-EU citizens. The bored guard in the third line for citizens kept chasing away people with the wrong passport. Asian passengers with duffel bags made a commotion, and the caterpillar line barely moved. But Shershnev stood calmly, having to rebuke his partner a few times with a frown for giving a woman in a hijab dirty looks.

Shershnev thought about the photographs taken by the surveillance people. The agents were sent from the embassy of a neighboring country which had done away with borders within the EU. They came and reported that they had done a clean job, no one noticed them, no counterintelligence activity had been noted, there were no bodyguards, the risk was minimal. The subject had not been seen. But inside the house—the security system was standard and easy to turn off—they found letters from the hospital. The subject was being examined and should be home soon.

He pictured the photographs taken by drone. The house on the edge of the forest. A deserted road. An ideal place, an easy place. No neighbors, no one would see, no one would find out. A hermit hidden in a secluded corner, setting his own trap.

The line had turned into a gypsy camp that seemed to have been there for years. The habit of a migrant life, of long, pointless waiting in crowded corridors in front of shut doors where your fate is being decided—that habit shaped people who had been so distinct forty minutes ago into a faceless conglomeration, an irrational but sensitive organism.

A rustle of movement, whispers—two yawning, grumpy border guards came and opened two more booths. The human porridge separated, with part flowing in their direction, stopping at the yellow line to wait their turn. Shershnev, who had noticed the men coming before anyone else, did not change his place. He did not like altering his decisions. A service psychologist called it passivity. But Shershnev knew the psychologist was wrong. He had always lacked that bit of agility, plain old luck, that lets people catch a train at the last moment and guess which line will move faster than others. If he started scurrying about, it made things worse, and the new line did not move at all and the train left from a different platform.

So he waited.

In a half hour, the crowd began to dissipate. A young couple went to the left booth, a stylishly dressed elderly man with a briefcase went to the right. Grebenyuk and he were next.

Shershnev had thought the old man and the couple would go through quickly—they usually don't hassle people like that. But the couple didn't have printouts of their return tickets, and the guard frowned and demanded all their hotel reservations. The man was also stuck, pointing at some paper in a plastic cover, instantly losing his glossy countenance and turning into an uncertain, intimidated supplicant.

The border guards were talking to one another. The crowd was shoving Shershnev. The sharp corner of a suitcase hit his anklebone hard. For a second, he thought this was a set up. Someone would grab him from behind, twisting his arm, while the idiot with the suitcase would pull out an automatic pistol. He suppressed the bad feeling.

Click, click, click—the magical sound of passports being stamped.

The metal doors opened. The old man left right away, and Grebenyuk took his place. The couple was holding things up. The girl was stuffing papers back in her bag, she dropped a file and pages flew out. She crouched to pick them up. Shershnev waited with discipline. Even though he was supposed to cross the border together with his partner.

Airport workers in bright vests pushed two wheelchairs,

bypassing the line. Young black boys, just skin and bones, covered with blankets, were holding piles of messy papers in their laps.

Shershnev took a step forward. But the guard raised his eyebrows and motioned him to stop.

Grebenyuk left. The boys were wheeled to the booths.

The nearer boy had a clumsy, perhaps homemade, prosthesis sticking out of his worn pant leg. It was too small: the boy had grown, but not his artificial leg. "A land mine," thought Shershnev. "Could have been one of ours. Where are they from? Somalia? Libya? Angola? Sudan?" He was sorry the mine had gone off at such a bad time. Now the explosion that took place many years ago on a different continent was holding him up. The other foot was wearing a brand-new sneaker, limp, with a puffy running sole. Just like the ones Maxim was wearing the day they played paintball. A day so near and so far.

The agent left his booth, examined the boy, and started leafing through the papers with the boy's escort. Shershnev was the calmest person in the airport. The two men kept talking. The boy sat there, aloof, exhausted by the long flight. At last, the guard stamped a paper. The man in the vest pushed the wheelchair through. The officer waved to Shershnev: Come over.

Shershnev was prepared to give him his cover story. He had a new passport with a fresh visa. His first entry. Questions were possible, almost inevitable. But the guard, as if in apology—or perhaps as a reward for the passenger's patience—ran the passport through the scanner, flipped through the pages and stamped it neatly, in the corner.

The door opened, and Shershnev stepped into the world he

had left decades ago, when he went back home to go to military school.

His father was commander of a communications platoon. Shershnev grew up in an army garrison that had taken over the old nineteenth-century barracks of a cavalry regiment that died out in World War I. He had hoped to return there to join his mother and father after his studies, to be in a special army group in the GDR. He would serve in intelligence, face-to-face with the enemy, on the farthest edge, where you could see the white column, crowned with a faceted cupola, of the American listening station on Devil Mountain.

It turned out differently. His parents came to him. The garrison left its barracks. They brought tanks, rockets, and other supplies on trains. The army, without suffering a defeat, was nevertheless retreating to the East.

His father, who had been awarded an order in 1968 for helping to suppress the Prague Spring with Operation Danube, never could accept the troop withdrawal. The treachery. The collapse of the impoverished army. The forced move to the reserves. He drank himself to death at the dacha he bought with the money he had saved while serving abroad, amid the apple trees that would not bear fruit on the poor, peaty soil. Shershnev would have been very happy for his father to see him now.

He was coming back.

While departing Moscow, their baggage, unexamined, was deposited in the cart with the luggage of the other passengers. The baggage for the flight had long been unloaded now. Suitcases from Hurghada circled on the lone working carousel.

Grebenyuk learned that their flight had been unloaded on carousel four. He found the piled-up suitcases. Shershnev's was not among them. They walked around the baggage claim area once again. Empty.

There were a dozen people at the Lost and Found counter. Shershnev recognized people from his flight: there was the bratty girl and her parents; there was the couple whose documents were spilled at passport control.

The counter was closed. No schedule, no notice. According to some cleaning person, the staff would come at five in the morning. Shershnev and Grebenyuk exchanged a look.

In principle, there was nothing in the suitcase of critical importance for the operation. Just everyday clothing, sensibly selected, good quality, and inconspicuous. Shershnev had proposed traveling without any luggage, even if it did not fit their image of guys on vacation looking for beer, girls, and presents. They needed only a few days. Then they would get back home. Nobody would care about the details of their cover stories. If they did, that meant the operation had gone south.

Despite the pressure and haste, they were outfitted more than adequately, good for months or years. The bosses had played it very safe, hedging their bets in case the operation failed. Now Shershnev felt that the loss of the suitcase was a good thing, as if all the additions, embellishments, and last-minute instructions were gone along with it. He taped his luggage tag to the counter, writing the name of his hotel on it. Let them send it, if they find it, they wouldn't be there anymore.

Two people at the Green Corridor. A tubby man busy with his cell phone. A thin blonde, clearly his senior, was adjusting her badge. Shershnev walked slightly ahead and to the left, setting himself up to be checked and covering his partner. The blonde let him through, and then called to Grebenyuk as he was almost past her.

Grebenyuk stopped. His English was poor, just enough to pass a test and get a raise. Shershnev had to interpret for him.

"Are you together?"

Shershnev nodded.

"How much cash do you have?"

"Four thousand euros." Shershnev obsequiously reached for his wallet.

"Open it." She pointed to Grebenyuk's bag.

He took it off his shoulder, laid it on the desk, and unzipped it. Shershnev checked the shiny panels of opaque glass in his peripheral vision; were there dark shadows of men in camouflage and masks, weapons ready? This was the best time to grab them, as they were the only four people in the corridor.

The fat man stopped staring at his phone and came over, blocking the way out. Grebenyuk was showing the customs officer his things. She pointed to his toiletry bag. Grebenyuk opened it unhesitatingly. The bottle glimmered in the light.

The woman looked at it with interest. She looked up at Grebenyuk. The major was of average height and big boned, dressed in expensive clothes, but still looked like a country hick who had been eating sunflower seeds and putting the shells in his pocket; he stood there quietly and calmly.

Shershnev's heart dropped to his feet. Only now did the disparity become apparent between the expensive cologne and Grebenyuk's appearance and the rest of the items in his bag.

Shershnev even imagined that she was sniffing the air to see if Grebenyuk was wearing that cologne.

Witch. She sensed something but could not tell where the deceit was; she was angry and she might even ask Grebenyuk to spray the bottle. Their instructions did not cover this possibility; everyone had been certain that the bottle would not attract notice. The technicians swore that the copy was exact, that even the manufacturer would not be able to tell, and that it weighed what the original did.

It was made by men, Shershnev thought. They could have messed up the color, using a similar shade instead of the correct one. They could have made a mistake in the ornate script. The female officer surely knew the duty-free assortment, she had a trained eye, and maybe her husband used that cologne. Or maybe her acute sense picked up on the container's special aura. After all, the glass was not made at the factory but in their special technical shop; different hands polished it, with other thoughts, with other aims. Witch.

Shershnev was figuring out how to distract her. Drop his bag? Say something?

"Ken ve go?" Grebenyuk asked, with a horrible accent and the supplicating simplicity of a confused foreigner scared by foreign customs.

The official, as if waking up, nodded automatically. Grebenyuk adjusted the things in his bag without haste. As he closed it, the zipper caught on fabric, he pulled it up and down and then tried to pull out the lining from the teeth. She turned away. Other passengers, cursing loudly about the airport service, entered the corridor. Grebenyuk threw his bag over his shoulder. Shershnev felt sharp needles pricking his hands.

"Dying for a piss," Grebenyuk said. "Where's the john here?"

They walked past the drivers holding signboards bearing names. The air was filled with the odors of unfamiliar food, tobacco, and car exhaust, which seemed to smell differently than back home.

In the toilet, Grebenyuk urinated noisily for a long time, while Shershnev couldn't start. It was only when Grebenyuk headed for the sink that the flow began from his penis. A cleaner came in, and Shershnev felt an overwhelming desire to knock over his cart, break the mop, and splash the bucket water on the walls.

He looked at himself in the mirror over the sink.

His face looked the same.

CHAPTER 11

Kalitin had dozed off in his favorite leather armchair by the fire. The smoky warmth and cognac had put him to sleep.

He dreamed that he was without flesh or memory and flying over a dark plain. He was soaring but he did not know his destination. The wind tossed him to the side, turned him upside down. Above him was emptiness, a malevolent sky without stars or planets. It was filled with visible wind, fluttering, flickering, like the potent milt of gigantic flying fish.

A wave crashed below. The dull arrow of a river showed him the way. He flew and his flight stirred the water. The bewhiskered catfish, at the bottom for the night, and the spotted burbots awoke from their sleep; so did the golden pheasants in the rushes.

A school of fish, his flock, swam behind him. Roe deer and hares, jackals, foxes, wolves, and boars ran along the banks—up, up, against the current, against gravity.

The stars lit up, gathering strength. Strange lights of imaginary constellations: Hour Glass, Owl, Scepter, Sphinx, Rat. Where the Milky Way lay in the old world the constellation of the Snake extended glowing green and red; the Snake was wrapped around the bowl of the firmament, the bowl of the universe.

As he flew, homeless, his memory returned—distant, cherished. He remembered how he was born in a transparent vessel, in the midst of shining whiteness and light; voices called him by name, joyous voices of gods dressed in white, celebrating his birth.

But the gods immediately hid him in dark confinement, until someone released him. He dissipated, dissolved, got lost among dead smells cut off from their source, among yesterday's shadows. But he did not vanish fully, because he was inherently alien to the world and it could not accept and dissolve him completely.

Then the gods called him again. He revived from dispersal and was filled to the brim with himself; like a raindrop plummeting to earth, he raced toward the distant call.

He flew above the river. The end of his journey was near. In the middle of the waters rose the enormous, the great Island, with searchlights running like lunar fingers through the dark. Fish leaped out of the water, dropping sparkles from their scales. Myriad animal eyes glowed in the dark of the forest and fields. The river retreated into its depths, revealing the Island's foundation cliffs, covered in waterweeds. He slid down, growing smaller, thickening; flowed in a stream down the chimney, penetrated bars and filters, and then dove into the light from the lamp, the sun of the lab. In its encircling glow, he drew himself into the desired, soothing cradle, the narrow opening of a test tube. He filled it and lay still.

The journey is done. He is home.

Kalitin woke up. His hand was on the neck of the cognac bottle. His head was foggy, even though he had not drunk a lot. The last coals were burning down. He added logs and fanned the flames. He rarely remembered his dreams in detail, only the ones that literally reflected reality. Now he remembered only remnants of the breeze over vast spaces, a faint trail leading to the Island.

Daydreams about the Island were his favorite emotional sustenance. The Island was his true birthplace. Recalling it, a place of strength and power, brought Kalitin a dull, sated drowsiness, as if these weren't incorporeal images but real food, rich, harmful, but satisfyingly delicious, like the boar hams served at the restaurant outside town by the old water mill.

Kalitin worried that one day the daydreams would stop nourishing him, reanimating him, encouraging him. They would just be memories, tasteless, useless, a burden. He tried to limit himself. After all, he had managed to quit smoking on doctor's orders and now only drank moderately!

But now, after his diagnosis, there was no point in postponing or hoarding the pleasure. He intended to take his tested remedy, have a feast, overindulging in the Island, the things that had given him a powerful, narcotic sense of immortality within the limits of life and beyond them, to stifle the banal, flat sense of death, to gain at least a week, a day, to awaken his strength so that he could reverse his fate and affirm hope for salvation.

Kalitin poured more cognac. He prepared to remember. In the flicker of the flames, embroidered with the golden stitches of sparks, he saw the blushing gelatinous surface of the river at sunset. In the dark spots between the tongues of fire, the secret part, the hidden second nature, he recognized the duality of his gift.

He drank, taking delight in himself remembering, creating a symphony, a mystical cosmogony of the Island, which had predetermined their connection, their preordained dependence on each other.

The Island's history began long ago. The mighty river destroyed the limestone ridge in its way. Inside it were hidden fossilized growths of coral; lily blooms on articulated stems, falling apart into rings; brachiopods like lacquer powder compacts. The river had washed away the limestone, leaving only one hill of the ridge that did not give in to the water surrounding it. Trees grew there, animals moved into the stone dens, and birds wove nests in the overhangs and slopes.

The very first people to find the Island avoided living there, even though it had convenient, deep caves. Located in the middle of turbulent waters, isolated, closed, menacing—it was only during the greatest droughts, which occurred every ten years or so, that there was a narrow path to it—the Island had been created by nature as a place for solitude, otherworldly, for meeting higher powers.

People built temples on the Island. It had seen tubby stone gods of the Paleolithic, gods of clay and of bone, carved wooden statues.

Then came monks forcibly baptizing local tribes. They dug out and burned wooden idols that did not have the strength to protect themselves and the faith.

The monks chopped down the sacred tree, the only oak on the Island, old, crooked, its roots deep in the yellow stone, and in its place built a chapel. They burned the former gods of linden and ash and threw the coals into the water. They could not break or move the ancient altar stone, washed in blood, a granite boulder alien to the region, which had been brought by unknown people to the Island from the north—by unknown means: barge, sledge over the ice; so it lay in the middle of the Island, like a dead but imperishable god.

The chapel was the start of the fortress monastery that defended the edge of the state from nomads, guarded the natural border that divided forest from steppe; many fervent prayers rose beneath its vaulted ceiling for the government and troops. Then the steppe was conquered, although it exploded with wild rebellions more than once.

The monastery expanded, built from the stone on which it stood. Above soared churches, belfries, chambers, walls, towers. Below, the paths of the quarry multiplied, descending ever deeper, turning into cellars, cells, storerooms, and crypts with the relics of the deceased recluses who had given the monastery its fame.

Also there, in the deepest reaches of the lower Island, where there was only the slow time of stone, forcibly tonsured prisoners lived and died, exiled, stripped of all secular disguises, former names, actions, and destinies. They knew only years—in spring the high river water seeped into the cells; the stone bore their notches; blind writing snaked along the walls in a chronicle of darkness, despair, faith. The upper, reigning Island founded its growing strength on them, the nameless men buried alive; it grew on the slow, meager, angry yeast of their suffering.

Then the lower levels were emptied. The former cells collapsed, burying the past. Prisoners were kept in the casemate above, built on the headland back in the days when ships plied the river under sail and robber gangs caroused on vessels propelled by oars.

The Island was no longer on the frontier of the empire, which had pushed back its borders to the seas and oceans, conquering many languages. These languages were heard in the prison cells—the languages of rebels, languages of freedom, now accompanied by the clanging of shackles.

They buried the prisoners on the headland. Limestone crosses of a different ritual, names in a different alphabet. The frosts, rains, and fogs ate away the stone, erasing letters and numbers. Scratched lines remained on the cell walls: poets' verses, scientists' blueprints, officers' vows.

By then the river was traveled by grain barges and paddle steamboats carrying passengers with a colorful sprinkling of hats and umbrellas.

The monastery was getting fat on the relics of its saints, on the prayers and money of travelers, peasants, and aristocrats. An icon appeared, allegedly found by monks near the water during a storm. A new church with five golden cupolas, visible for twenty versts along the river, was built for the icon. An artist among the monastery novices, a young talented master who had grown up just in time among the brethren, ornamented it with paints he created, made of substances found only in the region. The painting was not bright. But it was clearly inhabited by the inexplicable mystery of the close interconnection of all existence, divinity and humanity. The monastery fishermen caught sturgeon in nets, the apprentices boiled fish glue that gave the paint a bonding strength, and the image lay on the rough, porous stone as if it were an intrinsic part of it, an expression of what was inside.

The monastery was preparing to celebrate the anniversary of its founding. A church historian wrote a book; its rough drafts, which had absorbed many old secrets, remained in the monastery library. The photographer who made jubilee postcards for the festivities left a catalogue of his photos in the library. It included views of the famous icon, its angels and saints, earthly mountains and heavenly heights.

These books and photos remained the primary testimony to the monastery's past. For the wave that engulfed the unassailable Island had come.

Landowners' estates blazed in early autumn along the banks, beyond the low forests. When the river iced over, dark military coats, sheepskin jackets, and homespun clothes appeared on the white snow. The ice, still thin, sang, groaned, howled—the howl of saw blades, bridge trusses, stretched wires, ship hulls in a storm. Men came with rifles and pitchforks and with them a horrible soul-shattering cloud of sound gathered over the Island, and the deep bell sounding alarm from the belfry drowned and faded in it.

For the first time since pagan days blood was shed openly on the Island and bodies were thrown in the river without cover. The monks and priests were killed or exiled.

Soon the Island returned to one of its previous secret forms: it became a prison. A concentration camp. A rebellion was suppressed in the nearest town. The officers of the old army were brought to the Island. The breaks in the old walls were bound with barbed wire, guard towers were erected hastily, and Maxim machine guns, thirsty for water when fired, were mounted on wooden machine gun tables.

Then, when the White Army, allies of the prisoners, reached the river downstream, the Reds brought a barge that had been used for transporting grain and forced the prisoners into the hold, telling them they were being moved to a different place. They padlocked the trapdoors, a tugboat led the barge into the waterway, the deepest part, and opened the seacocks. The barge groaned beneath the water, its voice metallic, deep, horrible. Then it choked and drowned.

The summer brought drought, the worst ever seen. The Island seemed to come ashore. If you came close by rowboat, you could see the barge on the bottom, among the weeds and fish. Just a little more, it seemed, and it would appear, raising its tower and sloping sides above the water.

The drought burned the harvest, and what did manage to grow and what was left from the previous year was seized by soldiers sent from the cities. The famine drove people to eat people. They dug up old animal burial grounds, no longer fearing Siberian anthrax. That was when they took down the crosses and bells in the monastery and took apart the icon stands—allegedly to buy bread for the starving with church gold. The region died out and emptied.

The commission that seized the church gold also opened the crypts. It certified that the corpses had rotted and their saintly incorruptibility was a lie perpetrated by the church. They toured different cities with the skeletons, displayed them—look, here is the truth of materialism, the exposure of religion's intoxication; then the skeletons vanished, probably dumped into a distant, deep ravine.

A commune moved into the former monastery a year later: military orphans, homeless children. They scraped off the famous frescoes on the church ceiling. The teachers wanted to turn it into a House of Culture. But the children ran away from the commune, by land and by water, and the police tried to catch them at train stations and in cellars, in vain.

For a few years, the monastery was abandoned. Fishermen avoided the waters of the Island, remembering the barge and the corpses in the metal hold, which had rusted into tatters.

Then completely different people came to the Island. Truly new owners. They posted the land along the banks of the river. They took over the dead villages, the fields and groves in the lowlands, built barracks, a water tower, aerodrome, clubhouse, and warehouses. They cleaned out the former churches and old cells, reinforced the bars built into the stone, and built a sturdy pier. They renovated the guard towers and added some new ones.

The Germans needed a secret location, far from the victors in Versailles, from the eyes of spies and snitches, to continue their experiments with chemical warfare and prepare to replay the lost war. The Soviets would get formulas, technology, methods of use; results, tables, reports, a schooling for their scientists. There, by the river, in Europe's dark closet, both sides found what they needed: a remote place with a rich landscape, changeable climate, a large natural temperature range, in the high thirties centigrade in summer and up to minus forty in winter, so they could simulate using the substances in various theaters of war in various seasons. It was a location depopulated after the famine and with a citadel easily protected and controlled, the former monastery.

Kalitin always regretted that he had not been there; that he had not been alive, had not existed then.

He knew that most of the experiments of that time were obsolete a decade later. There was no cavalry, whose horses were to be stunned by clouds of gases. Airplanes flew three times faster, and aerosols were no longer suitable. New filters for gas masks, new damaging substances appeared. Most important, the World

War, which his country had won without recourse to the Island's creations, but with gunpowder and steel.

The joint experimental facility was closed in 1933. Soon after, the river was confined and artificial seas were created. Nearby cities were drowned, entire cities with houses, churches, sidewalks, and cemeteries; inconsolable ghosts of the past settled in its waters. The Island was supposed to vanish, too: the dam for their area existed only in the blueprints. It was not built because of the war.

When Kalitin looked at the photographs in the archive taken by Germans on the Island, which had been transferred to Europe and then returned—a horse in a gas mask, biplanes on the edge of a field, docks, a group shot in front of the lab building (every part of which he knew), the former church—he thought he was seeing paradise, an ideal conception of space and time.

In that world, most people did not yet see the dark side of science, its evil twin. Science was pure, even though it was already marked by its latest inventions at the Somme and Ypres. The blame was placed on the politicians and generals. The scientists were free and not subject to trial. In those days there were different weights accorded to morality that made exceptions for people of knowledge. And Kalitin yearned for the gravity that he'd never experienced.

He was born after millions had died in gas chambers and two of the German chemists in the group photo on the Island, captured by the Allies, were first sent to the defendants' bench and then to the gallows. Science, his path to power, was besmirched, publicly declared evil—evil in the eyes of the masses.

So Kalitin was forced to hide. Even without the death

sentence pronounced in his homeland, he could not openly declare who he was. There would be journalists scrambling after sensational stories, there would be articles about the Island of Death—or whatever name they came up with for it—calling for investigation and a trial. So Kalitin sometimes dreamed about the Island of long ago, as the ideal refuge, the inaccessible land of the blessed. But he was ready to return to his own, usual one.

When war broke out with Poland, they set up a concentration camp on the Island again and kept Polish prisoners there. Then, after the attack by Germany, there were German and Romanian prisoners from units shattered at Stalingrad. For some time only German officers and generals refused to collaborate. Then there were Japanese captured in the Far East. After a few years, the camp was empty, for the prisoners had been transferred to other places, ore mines and logging camps.

The Island was revived almost immediately, it was so good, so needed, so convenient. The Iron Curtain was lowered, the threat of a third world war was growing, and the old testing ground was back in business.

But now it was divided among several competing agencies. The arguments slowed down testing, led to mistakes and quiet sabotage, to scientific backbiting.

Uncle Igor, Igor Zakharyevsky, truly revived the Island. He had long wanted to leave the old City and found a new one: even more closed, equipped with cutting-edge technology, and subordinate only to him in science; it was his ticket to immortality, the chance to be elected a full academician on the secret list.

While Kalitin was in school, Zakharyevsky collected allies, led intrigues, pushed his idea at the very top. The result was the birth of a new unnamed city, known only by a number. All the sections divided up by bureaucratic battles were gathered into a whole. Uncle Igor made sure the future laboratory was classified top secret, which, as Kalitin knew better than most, since he later headed it, turned the Island into a black hole, a scientific domain free of all local and agency oversight, exempt from almost every kind of control.

Essentially, Zakharyevsky could work on whatever he wanted. None of his colleagues had the right or possibility to evaluate the quality of his programs, methods, and goals. Kalitin knew how prodigious sinecures arose, colonies of scientific drones, who worked for decades—until the top patron fell—on some expensive nonsense as long as it could be wrapped in the right slogans and appeared to follow the Marxist line; becoming encrusted in factories, vacation homes, polyclinics, but not bringing even a grain of knowledge.

Kalitin was also devoted to Zakharyevsky because he had not created the Island for the sake of fool's gold. They were both attracted to true knowledge that did not depend on the direction of the ideological wind; only such knowledge gave long-lasting power.

Zakharyevsky was supported by the KGB: where there are secrets, there are bonuses for concealment, new staff, control, operative work. Kalitin also suspected that the head of security on the Island, a former Stalinist general moved into active reserves, was also seeking a quiet, opaque harbor in the new unsettled times; he, or rather his colleagues from the old guard, helped Zakharyevsky.

Kalitin often imagined the Island as a *matryoshka* doll, consisting of layers of increasing secrecy.

The first, external layer was the country itself with its closed borders. The Island was not mentioned in reference books, the press, or radio, nor was it indicated on maps. An entire region was closed to foreigners. The American spy satellites—the Island had the schedule of their passing overhead, when outside work and field testing were not allowed—were supposed to see a maximum security prison.

Kalitin knew the neighboring settlements were filled with informers, that the Island was enmeshed in invisible security threads, surrounded by hidden sentinels; only the river was allowed to flow past unhindered. But the river was an ally, a guardian of secrets. The river protected the Island, and its images reflected in the water remained unrecognized. Tourist boats traveled along the far shore, where nothing could be seen through binoculars. Kalitin liked being part of the power that changed schedules and routes, a power that could bend time and space, so that the Island could remain just an island for outsiders: an almighty and all-pervading power.

Naturally, on the Island, which now had the status of a city spreading along the banks of the river, there were numerous degrees of proximity to the secret core, separated by fences, barbed wire, checkpoints, patrols, passes, nondisclosure agreements, and in-depth investigation of candidates. The periphery, the outline of the Island, could be seen from without, could be calculated from correspondence and financial documents.

But the closer to the core, the more illusory became the very existence of the inner Island, known to a contracting circle of the initiated. Only a few individuals knew about the laboratory, so covert that it did not exist on a single list of secrets.

All the previous reincarnations of the Island seemed to come together in the laboratory. It was sanctuary, prison, altar, and test ground. A new synthetic entity, an abstraction, cut off from the outside world. The laboratory.

His first sight of the Island was from the ferry. A late autumn sunset was busy over the river, and the Island appeared from clouds of fog, alien to everything, aloof, magical. Kalitin felt it was a sign, and he appreciated, understood, and fell in love with the Island at that moment, guessed all its features, advantages, obvious and hidden gifts—and was prepared to give his life to the power that had created the Island, because it was preordained for him, responded to the deepest desires of his being.

Kalitin was not a faithful Communist. He knew the clichés and rituals well, and had a party membership card—without it he would not have risen beyond laboratory head. Kalitin was attracted by the paradoxical freedom-in-prison that the Island offered in a land of ideologized, dogmatically mediated science.

He was a knowledgeable, intelligent chemist. No genius, compared to others. He needed that closed, hermetic world, in order to exist, to work. It did not have the gravity of morality, and he was able to rise to the heights of circumscribed genius by inventing Neophyte, the most perfect of his creations.

All of Kalitin's previous life was built on the idea of the Island's singularity. He knew it the way a mollusk knows its shell, and he carried it with him even when he was deprived of it. He knew that there were other closed cities, other refuges; but only the Island and Kalitin were inseparable. That inseparability was never doubted; even the house on the mountain slope he had come to love was only an imposed replacement, pathetic in comparison.

And suddenly—the fire had died down, the coals covered in gray ash—he felt that the Island was no longer unique.

Just as love contains the bitter seed of its own death as it matures, the total sense of merging with the Island brought an alien, unknown sensation; Kalitin realized, admitted, that he had been so devoted, so surrendered to it in vain. If not for that lulling, weakening loyalty, something else could have appeared in his life long ago.

For example, another Island.

The thought was almost blasphemous, but in it, despite himself, Kalitin felt the painful burn of hope.

His memory, as if agreeing to rejection and betrayal, offered up a contemporary appellation: bikini. Bikini Atoll. Atoll. Island.

Kalitin imagined it—a circular, palm-covered reef placed on an underwater volcano, surrounded by infinite ocean. The blue waters of the inner lagoon. The white, one-story laboratory building with heavy shutters against the sun—many substances do not like light, they need coolness and shade. A reliable dock for the delivery boats from the mainland. A four-legged tower with a roof, the silver finger of the searchlight dissolving in the night, dancing on the waves . . . After all, they—the fabulously wealthy—could do more than cure him. They could buy him an Island.

Island.

Island.

Island.

Kalitin's hands shook. The bottle knocked against the crystal glass and made it ring. He wept with tears postponed for two decades, no longer salty; belated, warm, ugly, desired.

CHAPTER 12

Shershnev opened the railway line magazine. He needed a distraction. An ad: a happy couple running along a white sand beach, a hammock, a bottle of wine, palm trees. Reduced fares on direct flights to Asia.

He was unhappy from the start with the travel plan imposed by the bosses and the cover story they provided. He would have done it fast, in one day. Fly in, complete the op, fly out. That's how the agents from the neighbors took out Vyrin.

But they came up with an allegedly touristic route for them—probably because of the scandal that followed Vyrin's death and the increased counterintelligence regimen. They land in one country, sort of coming in through the back door; travel to another country, rent a car there . . . It might be good for covering up their intention, but the route was too long and fraught with problems, missed connections, inevitable in travel.

And so it began. They had printed tickets for the train, car 2, seats 49 and 47. When the train pulled into the station, there was no car 2: 22, 23, 24, 25, 26, 27.

He ran with Grebenyuk to the locomotive: Maybe there was

another train right ahead? And then came the cars numbered in the twenties? No, the numbering started with car 22.

It wasn't a trap. Not a trick. Just the usual stupidity, a glitch in the reservations system. Shershnev saw the train was full and didn't know if they would be allowed to board with the wrong tickets. Back home he would have shown his ID and they would be found seats in business class. But here? What if they had to go get new tickets?

It all worked out, of course. The conductor apologized and told them to take any seat they could. But Shershnev couldn't get rid of the feeling that there was a weak but clear resistance to their mission, emanating from no one, coming out of nowhere. That happens in the spring sometimes, when you go out skiing in the morning and the snow starts getting sticky in the sunshine— not enough to slow the skis but enough to lose the smoothness and ease, and you need to exert more effort.

Shershnev knew that the subject had taken the same path many years ago. Allegedly on a business trip to negotiate the purchase of equipment. A delegation of a dozen or so. He probably would not have been allowed to go to America. Even in those lax times. But the subject traveled to a country that just a year or two ago had still been socialist. Where friendly security services were still in place; where Soviet intelligence had recently had not just a residency at the embassy but a full-fledged and, most important, legal presence. The subject moved into a hotel with the rest. He visited the manufacturing complex, had dinner with the group that evening. And he vanished during the night.

They established that he had gotten train tickets. Back then his route remained within the borders of one country. Today there were two states: they separated in 1993. No one knew whether the subject got off somewhere along the way or traveled to the end.

They were on the trail. The cold, scentless trail of the defector. Shershnev knew how to support and develop the connection between hunter and prey; he enjoyed shooting hares along the blacktop or chasing a fox. But now Shershnev did not want that connection to appear. He sensed that it was becoming two-sided, unlike his other missions.

He did not pity the subject and he was ready to execute the order. But he was beginning to understand him, since he had also lived in those ambiguous years and had experienced the same fear, when it seemed that the service he had just joined could be disbanded. He remembered the despair of his father who did not want to retreat, to remove the hammer and sickle badge from his cap, to change his military oath; the fear of informers afraid to inform, the fear of generals removed from staff, the fear of the recent coup plotters who ended up in prison. And that was nothing, there was even the fear of the guard dogs.

Shershnev understood clearly why the subject had defected. Yet that understanding was superfluous since it seemed to excuse the subject's action. Grebenyuk was only five years younger. Not having witnessed that moment of weakness in the omnipotent service, Grebenyuk would not experience such doubts.

In the end, Shershnev did not have doubts, either. He was merely musing, but these thoughts seemed dangerous to him, for he was used to controlling his reflections; Grebenyuk had surely been told to watch his partner and would later write a report—as would he himself. Shershnev tried to push away the unsummoned thoughts so that not even a shadow of them crossed his face.

When he read the circumstances of the subject's defection, Shershnev noted that some things were redacted. Not for secrecy, but because they created something like an alibi. Shershnev easily read between the lines, filling in the censored facts: the entire country was undergoing the same thing then and it was not hard to picture what had happened in the closed city.

Power outages. No more special food deliveries, empty shelves in stores. Delays in salary payments, which had turned into play money by then anyway. Talk that the closed city status would soon be removed. Paradise lost—they had been living there with everything done for them, unlike the entire country standing in lines.

More gaps in the wall around the city; they had stopped repairing it. Theft—from the workshops, from the lab. New companies, cooperatives, created by bosses embracing perestroika and grabbing up big pieces and crumbs for themselves. Cold radiators in winter.

According to the documents, the subject tried to adjust to the new life. A foreign commission on disarmament was allowed on the Island for the first time. They didn't see anything, they weren't allowed in the laboratory or the warehouses, but the fact itself was important. A trusted person reported that the subject tried to initiate contact with two of the inspectors. Both were known and there were reports on them.

The first was a real scientist and also a recruiter, who had been asked by interested Western firms to find suitable candidates, buy up some valuable brainpower, as well as do the inspection. The subject did not tell him what he really did, and the recruiter did not follow up.

The second was a real recruiter who had helped his country's intelligence. He focused on scientists working on top-secret topics. The old man opened up to him and they had a conversation. The deal was almost done. But the security department interfered and they began investigating the subject.

Here came the most interesting episode. Formally, there was enough evidence to charge him for revealing state secrets, for "treason to the homeland," which was then still subject to the death penalty. But the investigation was quickly ended. The old man got off with a reprimand—too easy even for those strange times.

Shershnev guessed the rest. A few months later a famous banker who knew the secret origins of some new fortunes was killed. The banker died quickly after a sudden collapse of his inner organs. The autopsy did not show poisoning, and the banker would have been buried if the investigators had not learned that his air conditioner had been repaired the day before; they found a small vial that was not part of the unit.

The case was reexamined three times, but never reached the courts. All the analyses were classified. The vial had been developed at the laboratory headed by the subject and was made for the remote use of exceptionally toxic substances; however, no trace of any substance was found. That was a trace in itself.

Pointing to Neophyte.

Untraceable and imperceptible—they were given a brief lecture on the contents of the vial.

It was obvious that the order had not come from the state, for then there would have been no investigation at all.

Someone had leaked the substance from the lab to the black market and it fell into the hands of amateurs. Rather, semiprofessionals who knew how to use it properly but failed to clear away the evidence.

A few months after the assassination, the subject, passive, used to life behind seven seals, and able to make contact only with two observers who had ended up on his doorstep, cleverly and efficiently made his escape. He took advantage of the security chief's vacation, handed the newbie deputy faked arrangements for his trip and ran off.

The triangle was coming together. The subject had been forced to give up the substance and then was blackmailed with a charge of revealing a secret. He was probably also paid, paid a lot—his product was invaluable. Then when an internal investigation of the murder was started, the subject got spooked. He realized they could make him the scapegoat. Or quietly get rid of him to keep him from giving evidence. He took the money and the product and got away.

Who could have blackmailed him? It must have been the security chief. A colonel, an officer of the active reserve, who had joined state security through Party selection from the manufacturing sector. He had a degree in technology. He was quite capable of orienting himself in these new conditions, figuring out just what he was guarding, trapping the subject, and organizing the sale. Conveniently, the security chief could blame the theft on Kalitin when he defected. That's probably why they allowed him to escape, Shershnev thought.

Wisely, Shershnev did not reveal any documented interest in the security chief. He thought he knew his name, a simple name like the ones given to them on their fake passports. He had seen it among other signatures on some secret agency document.

The former head of security, if he had returned from the active reserve, could be one of the people issuing the order to get rid of the subject.

That did not make the order illegal in Shershnev's eyes. He would have executed a personal order from the bosses, unconnected to the interests of the service. For example, he would have killed that banker. But now he was feeling unwanted sympathy for the subject. They were connected like sound and echo, like a pair of substances composing a binary poison. The scientist created a substance, Shershnev deployed it; they shared all the real work, took the risk. Shershnev sensed it was wrong for them now to be once again forced together.

Shershnev looked at Grebenyuk. The major was asleep, or pretending to be. Neat little houses flashed by the windows. The conductor was serving coffee from the restaurant car. He stood up to stretch, rolled his shoulders, and the young woman across the aisle—in good shape, she probably worked out—gave him an understanding smile. Shershnev saw his reflection in the window out of the corner of his eye; the man at whom the woman smiled. Suddenly Shershnev wanted to remain as that person, an unknown passenger traveling from Point A to Point B, to get off the train with her in a suburb. With the full brunt of his character, Shershnev attacked himself for that thought. He felt anger rising against the subject, who had somehow tricked him into compassion.

The conductor mumbled the station name. Grebenyuk opened his eyes. One more stop, and then the end. The destination. Prague.

CHAPTER 13

There was one more part in the beautiful epic of the Island, never completed for Kalitin, that he would happily have excluded. The final years. The chapter of collapse and betrayal. Black, unwanted pages. Kalitin tried not to remember them. But today one, the very first, came on its own.

He had been given a sign that the Island would no longer be the same. But Kalitin didn't see it, didn't understand its significance. Perhaps because the first to feel the underground din were not humans but animals—like the secret pulse of a coming earthquake that humans could not sense.

It was the Island's golden period, the zenith of its capabilities. Unfortunately, Zakharyevsky, its founding father, had died suddenly. And soon after, like a faithful dog, the old head of security died.

Kalitin became head of the main laboratory, the heart of the Island. He could not aim for Zakharyevsky's position due to his young age and administrative "weight." The nominal head was one of Zakharyevsky's deputies, a gray man strong in bureaucratic dealings; like that minion of the General Secretary Andropov who was half-dead but took the throne of his deceased master for a year. Everyone understood that Kalitin was next in line for the throne; it was a required exchange, an intermediate move.

The new security chief, the head Cerberus, seemed good to Kalitin at first. He had been friendly with the predecessor, but he had been a dinosaur, a relic of the cannibalistic times, who knew nothing about science. The new fellow represented a different generation; he had a degree in chemistry and let him know that he supported him, understood, would facilitate things and wanted to be friends.

It was the Island's golden time, the season to harvest glory. The closed city had grown. Thanks to Zakharyevsky's efforts, there were several more laboratories. New residential buildings were rapidly rising.

Research was conducted on a broad scale. Zakharyevsky had taken over several promising areas that were not exactly suited to the Island's original profile—well, so what, everyone took as much as they could, and Kalitin didn't have a problem with that.

The army was fighting for the umpteenth year in the East, bogging itself down ever deeper into a partisan war. The scientists were reading intelligence materials stolen from the United States about Korea and Vietnam; the distant hills in Afghanistan did not have jungles, so defoliants were useless, but the experience of smoking people out was helpful—out of caves, tunnels, culverts that the mujahedeen had turned into cover and supply lines.

The Island had specialists in air, atmosphere, and ventilation; architects, technicians, and speleologists working on what to release and how to release it into an enclosed space with a complex configuration so that the substance would easily be diffused with a natural or forced air stream without collecting only in the upper layers or precipitating only to the lower ones.

Kalitin made a proposal. It was effective but expensive. The military wanted something cheaper. They brought in a group of specialists in biological weapons and suggested holding comparative field tests. This was a crude violation, for the Island testing field was not intended for that kind of experimentation.

Zakharyevsky would have been able to fend them off. But they hammered his former deputy and got through him.

At the edge of the field, by the river, there were karst caves and sinkholes. Someone came up with the brilliant idea of doing the tests there in conditions that were exactly like the battle areas. They found two noncontiguous caves, sealed all the exits, measured the volume, set up compressors by the entrance, and ran the hoses. The outside specialists, who knew the economy and effectiveness of their substances, were certain they would succeed. The idea was to seal the caves after the substances were pumped in and open them the next day, sending a team in hazmat suits to tally results.

They trucked in the monkeys. Usually the experienced soldiers guarding the zoo culled the most violent and the weakest, shooting them. But here they used them all—the military wanted a large-scale experiment, and the lab didn't want to waste its best material on an experiment that might interfere with their own project.

The monkeys were pushed into the caves and then they waited an hour. They assumed the primates needed time to find levels and holes for themselves, and then they started pumping. The generals, professors, the entire retinue were ready to leave.

The tables were set at the Island hotel and the steam baths were heated in the cottages. A yellow cistern of beer—an Island specialty—was cooling in a special chamber, and waitresses and women skilled in revelry, brought in by the security department, were waiting.

The alarm was raised by Lieutenant Kalimullin, an old-timer on the Island, commander of one of the guard units, a steppe dweller by lineage and the nature of his wild soul, who considered the Island supernatural. He once brought Kalitin—for no concrete reason—some steppe foxes caught in a snare, shedding, bald, vicious, gnawing at the bars of the cage.

Kalimullin pulled his machine gun off his shoulder, fired the obligatory shot in the air, and then aimed at something in the distance. As the lieutenant later recounted, at first he thought some people had gotten into the testing ground and were headed to the wire fencing. Someone with sense at the nearest watchtower turned on the projector and ran the spotlight over the karst sinkholes—it was getting dark, the technicians had spent a lot of time plugging in the compressors and making sure things were hermetically sealed—and in the bouncing light they saw five monkeys running to the fence, swaying, but—so it seemed to Kalitin and not only him—supporting one another, like wounded soldiers unwilling to surrender.

Kalitin understood at once. The soldiers—dolts, jackasses—had not checked the caves properly and had missed a crack. Or maybe the monkeys had dug themselves out, the land was friable, soft, the limestone washed away.

No one had made maps of the underground passages. They had measured by sight. And now tried to figure out where the fugitives were coming from: the cave where they were testing Kalitin's substance, which was not contagious, or the cave full of the army's poison—in which case the monkeys could be walking biological weapons. They hadn't died yet, but that didn't mean anything, the virus could be in their blood.

Kalimullin, good old Kalimullin, was already shooting in short bursts. One monkey fell, then another. They were having problems with the machine gun on the tower: it must have gotten stuck. The men who were armed took guns out of their holsters.

The fence was supposed to stop them, the barbed wire was high tension. But Kalitin sensed failure and realized something incredible would happen. Where the wire lay along the edge of a karst sinkhole, one monkey pushed another. It fell and burned in a violet flash. Two others slipped outside, as if they knew the short circuit would make the bottom row of the barbed wire safe.

Amazingly, no one panicked, Kalitin recalled, even though they all understood that they could lose not only their army and civilian rank, but their heads as well. The old general, who had taken Königsberg as a senior sergeant and had commanded a regiment in 1956 in Hungary, activated the closest garrison—allegedly for an unplanned training session. They used secret telephone lines to reach a zoologist in Moscow, the best specialist in primates. He didn't understand the question at first—where will a monkey run to hide in the conditions of central Russia?—but then, after the general roared out a concise and useful description of the locale, the specialist commanded them somewhere unexpected: not into the woods but into the rushes, into the marshes.

So the wild hunt began. They were under the spell of primitive thirst for revenge. Motorboats rushed up and down the river, searchlights checking the river reaches, scaring off fishermen from favorite spots. Cars raced along the banks, twin beams of headlights bouncing, and helicopters buzzed overhead. Military trucks spread out in a wide arc, dropping off groups at inter-sections with instructions to canvass residents about anything unusual and moving out in search parties. The soldiers either joked or moved in silence, obeying the strange order: find and destroy a monkey, the reward a medal and ten days' leave, and for privates—sergeant's stripes.

Crackling voices and static came over the walkie-talkies. They had already driven away two fishermen. They wounded a thief stealing kolkhoz hay. Two trucks collided, six wounded.

Voices interrupted their communications: the police, the second secretary of the oblast party committee, even some bum from the fishery management office, who somehow got on the closed line—What's going on?

The generals pressured them with their big stars, insisted on secrecy, sent them to the commander of the *okrug* for information. The helicopter shook, Kalitin wanted to throw up. They dragged him into the Mil copter, as if to demonstrate that they were all in the same boat. The pilots were just back from Afghanistan, the very mountains where the army planned to cleanse the caves, and now they were showing off, practically shaving the tops of trees with their propeller, hugging the dark water, sliding the belly along the craggy banks, and chasing an untended flock into the night—the fat white sheep scattered in every direction. The copi-lot laughed—he should have taken one for shashlik, but there was no time to land.

The airwaves whistled after midnight: got 'em. The copter

dropped, making a U-turn, and howled as it accelerated. They landed, creating waves, on a stony spit. The soldiers ran into the night and using a waterproof sheet—another smart command—carried in a twisted body powdered with chlorine, as if with white snow. Strawberry pink spots of blood appeared on the chlorine. No gas masks, no protective gear, no time to put them on—only the desperate hope that the monkeys were from Kalitin's cave, had sensed the stinking, powerful chemicals, huddled in a far corner and accidentally found a way to the surface.

Kalitin took the blood sample himself; a Mi-2 helicopter flew to the laboratory with it.

Then there was another flight, and Kalitin could no longer tell if he or the propellers were spinning. A signal from the other direction, thirty kilometers away. A spurt of the helicopter on its last liters of fuel. A heavy landing. A pale, hungover dawn. Lieutenant Kalimullin's predatory, triumphant face. A long narrow break in the rushes, the slurp of smelly stagnant water, and there at the end, on broken reeds, a deformed monkey cut down by a long burst of bullets. The first one, the one that had led the others and had knocked one into the electric fence. It had almost made it through the last ring, but Kalimullin up on a cliff saw movement in the rushes and shot from afar, counting on luck rather than accuracy.

Kalitin barely held back the nausea. For a second he thought they had killed the ancestor of all humans. Kalimullin's shooting had been guesswork, he couldn't see what was in the rushes, ape or man, a stranded poacher, for instance.

The hunters stood quietly, drained. They cupped lit cigarettes in their hands, warming their chilled fingers.

Kalimullin recognized the monkey, a large combative male with a torn left ear. The male had been in the cave pumped with Kalitin's chemicals. He thought that the ape must have swallowed some of the substance and it had worked; the bullets finished what the gas had begun.

No one celebrated the salvation, no one cursed out loud— dozens of armed men, exhausted by the night's work.

The helicopter remained on the bank. They promised the pilots a tanker barge would come for them. They returned in Kalimullin's open-top jeep. They tossed the dead animal wrapped in a tarp into the trunk.

The driver, worn out, drove carefully but still managed to hit potholes. Kalimullin frowned but said nothing. It was this sergeant who drove the car up the hill, reversed, and braked so that the lieutenant could fire his successful round. Next to Kalitin in the back seat dozed Kazarnovsky, senior scientific fellow of his laboratory.

Some time back, Zakharyevsky chose him to partner with Kalitin, but Kazarnovsky did not live up to expectations, he did what he was told, no more. Twice he had asked for a transfer, and the chief of security informed Kalitin that Kazarnovsky had twice made suspicious requests to the special section at the institute library for books that did not always entirely correspond to his research topic; for example, a foreign scientific encyclopedia volume requested by Kazarnovsky allegedly for its article on structural modeling also contained an article on Andrei Sakharov.

Actually, Kalitin was less bothered by Kazarnovsky's half-hearted dissident behavior—he defended it to the security chief— than by his passivity. After all, their late patron Zakharyevsky was a very ambivalent ideological communist. There were times he said outright treasonable things, knowing that the room was probably monitored. But how Zakharyevsky worked! He was forgiven all for that, and that's why Kalitin respected him so much; Kazarnovsky was a wimp.

They drove a long time, wandering on bad country roads. Kalitin looked around with unexpected interest; essentially, this was the first time he had seen the areas around the Island, the life of ordinary people outside the protected territory. The harvest was in, the fields were empty, with birds pecking at the last of the grain. Smoke rose from the chimneys in villages. Thousands of ordinary, sad sounds of life, forgotten by Kalitin, came from them. Lulled by the sounds, he daydreamed. He thought that they had just saved this sweet, peaceful life from an enemy threat, and that all their efforts ensured that stoves would burn, dogs would bark, well water would pour into empty buckets, and sleepy children would get ready for school.

He awoke near a village general store. Kalimullin stopped to get something for breakfast. The store had just opened, but there was a line outside, waiting for the bread truck to unload.

The lieutenant and his driver waved away the outraged women and went inside. The dusty and branch-whipped jeep was surrounded by curious boys. They should have been at school at that hour, but apparently the mothers had sent them for groceries or kept them with them, so that they could get bread and grain for two.

Kalitin felt uncomfortable. The pushy women, the noisy, grumbling line, the obnoxious kids annoyed him. The boys suddenly ran off and whispered to the adults, pointing at the car.

Kalitin turned around and saw that the bouncing ride had loosened the tarp. The sun shone on the monkey's dead face, yellow teeth bared in the pink mouth; shiny chrome-green flies crawled over the black fur.

Kalitin knew from the regular reports of the security department that the locals remembered many things. For instance, the Germans who had worked there before the war—some of the old men in the village had worked hauling water, others had been carpenters in the barracks. There were also rumors in the area that the bulldozers digging foundation pits for new buildings opened up holes filled with bones, both animal and human. Other rumors maintained that on the Island they made zombielike soldiers from dead criminals. The rumors were faithfully reported by informers.

Kalitin considered them amusing, a rudiment of the archaic peasant mind. He knew for certain that no bones had been dug up by bulldozers and no supersoldiers were created in the labs. Of course, he was surprised that despite all the secrecy measures, information still leaked out in a thin stream, as if these backward people had their own informers—animals, birds, dew, trees, grass. But that was the guards' problem. He liked the image of the mysterious, terrifying citadel that wielded power over the region. It would be a shame if the locals knew nothing at all. It would remove some zest from his life.

But now Kalitin was wary. The people had crowded together, whispering. Trouble emanated from their poses, their faded clothing, weary faces, neutered figures that had lost male and female characteristics, retaining only the traces of heavy labor.

Faces, faces—Kalitin suddenly saw them in extreme

proximity, screaming about the hidden pains of their bodies, stretched, squashed, asymmetrical, with hairs on warts, bushy eyebrows above dead eyes. The faces mocked him, danced around the car, peered into his pupils, bared yellow pointy teeth, like the monkey's.

"That's our work, you know," Kazarnovsky said calmly, his tone cool.

Kalitin noticed what he meant.

At the end of the line were a mother and daughter. The girl had a bloated, lumpy figure, faded eyes with huge whites, thin grayish hair. Her heavy body was poised on thin, bird-like legs, toes without nails visible through the torn straps of her sandals.

"That's just an illness," Kalitin replied, trying to sound indifferent. "You're tired."

"Just an illness?" Kazarnovsky asked loudly, too loudly. "The girl's around four. Four years ago they repaired the filtration system of the exhaust ventilation. Remember? They took off the old filters but did not replace them. The suppliers messed up the invoice. Zakharyevsky ordered the testing to continue. According to the prevailing winds, everything would be scattered above the river. We were inside. The exhaust fan blew everything away from us. That continued for two weeks. There's your damned prevailing winds. Look. Look around you!"

If not for the night that drained his strength, Kalitin would have cut off his subordinate on the spot. But Kalitin sat there like a sack. Kazarnovsky had energy somehow, as if he was getting it from the people in line, the dead ape, the rising sun.

His words had turned the world inside out, revealing the hidden side. Kalitin no longer saw the pastoral landscape, the glowing light of life, the healthy flesh of the universe, but the dark spots of diseases, the ulcers of postponed death sprinkled on the foliage, in people's bodies and faces, in the crooked letters of the *GROCERY* sign, in the potholed asphalt, in the cracked windowpanes of listing huts.

"I don't know about the enemies, but we're doing a very good job of destroying ourselves," said Kazarnovsky. His voice trembled.

Kazarnovsky turned away and froze in a tense pose.

If he could, Kalitin would have killed him then. But Kalitin's vision was still blurred by the dark spots of death: the whole world was mottled, as if eaten by black aphids.

Kalimullin and the driver came out of the store. The crowd calmed down at the sight of military uniforms. Everyone looked only at the head of the person in front. The lieutenant handed Kalitin half a loaf of freshly baked bread and a bottle of milk; Kalitin dove into the fragrant mass, swallowing without chewing and washing it down with milk. A rich stream dribbled into the collar of his checked shirt.

"What's the matter with him?" Kalimullin asked directly, all distinctions erased by the hunt.

"He's faded," Kalitin replied. "Nerves shot."

Kalimullin shook Kazarnovsky with unexpected ease—he must have come from a big family where he took care of the little ones, Kalitin thought enviously—and handed him the second half of the loaf and a bottle. Kazarnovsky started drinking and chewing. Obeying his lingering hatred, Kalitin threw out the still-warm crust onto the road; he did not want to share bread with the enemy. With a traitor.

Kalitin did not inform on him. It would have been unwise by his lights. First you inform voluntarily, then they ask you to do it. He did not like being in a dependent position.

Kalitin got rid of him swiftly, elegantly, by someone else's wish. The Chernobyl nuclear power plant exploded, and a coded message came to the Island: send specialists to work in the contamination zone. Everyone in their lab, where they experimented with radioactivity, understood the risk. That was when the director of the institute selected Kazarnovsky, on Kalitin's suggestion. He quoted the coded message demanding the most qualified specialists loyal to the Party. Immediate departure, the AN-24 turboprop was waiting at the airport. The aim and location of the trip could not be revealed to the family. Kazarnovsky stood up, round-shouldered, weary, and calmly thanked those gathered for their trust. He walked past the long counter, followed by dozens of eyes, met Kalitin's stare, nodded briefly, almost imperceptibly, and went out the door.

The union head later sent someone to visit him in the radiology hospital; to bring flowers, fruit, some extra food. But while they were getting approval for the visit and organizing it, Kazarnovsky died.

He should not have been exposed to a fatal dose; he knew all the norms and calculations. He volunteered to save others and spent too much time in the "hot zone." It took time to get him to the hospital, for the doctors to attend to him.

Kazarnovsky was buried in a sealed lead coffin. Kalitin even made a speech. After all, he had been a fairly good scientist.

After that death, everything went haywire. A fire in the lab held up research for at least a year. Problems with delivery of lab mice—Lord, they couldn't find mice in the country! Vera's death.

Yes, Vera's death—Kalitin played the list of obligatory memorial phrases through his head, a shorthand transcript of the grief he never felt.

He would have forgotten his unloved wife long ago. Erased the circumstances of her death from his memory. But he couldn't. Her death was forever linked to the main moment of his life—the creation of Neophyte. As if Vera had paid his debt with her life.

CHAPTER 14

I wonder if the subject knew his wife was an informer, thought Shershnev.

He was with Grebenyuk in a beer hall, eating pig knuckles with sauerkraut. They had two steins each: the beer was light and begged to be drunk. It would be bliss to down five or six, but they had to drive tomorrow.

If he were alone, Shershnev would have done it. What could happen to him? It was a good place, even if it was for tourists; no overcharging or crowds. Grebenyuk would have drunk that much for sure. But they were together, and each had to write a report about the other's behavior. Shershnev felt that if he had suggested it, Grebenyuk would support him. He was a regular guy and would not do him dirt later. But sometimes it doesn't work out, something is not quite right. So you just sit there fondling your glass.

I'll bet he didn't guess, Shershnev continued thinking. That was a pleasant thought. It put the subject in his place; it aroused the lieutenant colonel's vanity in a petty, tipsy way. They set the dope up with a pleasant lab assistant, clever and loose, and he fell for it. The lab assistant had been working for the security apparatus since college.

What worried, even upset Shershnev, was that he couldn't decide whether her reports could be trusted. Formally—yes. She wrote frankly and did not protect her husband. She could have softened a few things. Even so, decades later, from a different time, Shershnev thought he was reading a diligently edited, clean copy, not lying but omitting. As if Vera, whose agent name was Housewife, had decided: it was better for her to have this vacancy than someone else who could really harm him. She pulled a fast one. In some sense, she sacrificed herself. Did she actually love her husband? Or does it just seem that way?

That impression pained Shershnev. He believed in the service's ability to tame, break, see through anyone. To get to the unconditional truth by force, if necessary. And here he came upon someone's faulty work long ago, the laziness or stupidity of the man who ran Housewife.

They left the beer hall. The lane led to the square.

Grilled sausage stands—delicious! Pushers huddled on the corner. A police car drove by. It was the peak of the evening, people had eaten and were headed for the bars.

"He did it here somewhere," Grebenyuk said, looking around. "When our tanks came in. Poured gasoline over himself and lit it. They called it a protest against the Soviet invasion. I keep thinking, why? Tanks don't care. At least throw a grenade . . . I read about it on the train," he explained, seeing Shershnev's confusion. "He's a national hero now. Let's go get some girls?" Grebenyuk asked without a pause, without transition.

"I'm not in the mood," Shershnev replied. He really wasn't.

Grebenyuk nodded, even though he must have thought that

the lieutenant colonel would also go out seeking entertainment, but preferred doing it alone.

Shershnev grimaced inside: good thing he didn't mention it over dinner. A discovery. Grebenyuk was a technician, they were trained differently. That incident was used as an example at their service school: a provocative act done under the influence of enemy propaganda. There was another such incident in Lithuania. In Kaunas. Amazing, he even remembered the formulation. The teacher explained that self-immolation, even if it seems unintentional, accidental, has to be investigated thoroughly, searching for the subjective.

Odd, Shershnev had forgotten completely that it had taken place here.

Grebenyuk, assured that his boss did not mind, turned behind a kiosk and immediately vanished among the passersby. Shershnev continued walking. He wanted to end this unnecessary, intervening day as fast as possible; in the morning they would rent a car, and everything would happen tomorrow.

Tomorrow.

He went into a store that was open late. He glanced at the windows, picked out a jacket, went into the dressing room, and then abruptly pulled back the curtain. No one.

He was sure they weren't being followed anyway. They were clean. But he still felt a weak, strange tension that increased with Grebenyuk's departure, a whisper of danger. Why did that idiot bring up the suicide? A bad sign. The devil made him do it.

He went back outside. Two tramps fighting by the garbage. Shershnev went around them in disgust—and suddenly grew wary, pulled himself together, without knowing why.

A woman.

A woman up ahead. By the ice-cream stand.

Shershnev saw her from the back.

Danger.

Danger emanated from her body, alien here where elderly people were usually trim, thin, and if they were fat, it was the amiable heaviness of gluttony.

A heavy but powerful body. You can move it or go around it; she will stand there, forcing you to notice her.

If ten of these women gather, a communal force develops the likes of which he did not perceive in women of his homeland. In Russian women he knew the power of humiliation, grief, prayer. But these mountain women had the power of impersonal unity, fearlessness born of disdain, a power that bewilders armed men. Not the hysterical-hypnotic power of gypsies, but that of witches, of ravens. Their everyday black dresses, heavy floor-length skirts, granny sweaters with peeling buttons, black or gray vests, woolen scarves. One breed, for him, a foreigner—one face, one voice capable of an unbearable screech that cuts like a saw; a scream with emotion, without relation to words; a pure sound against which there is no immunity. That scream can force a cordon of men behind metal shields to retreat, can turn soldiers into boys.

Shershnev imagined he heard that scream.

Like that morning after the night spent interrogating the boy in the shipping container on the base in Chechnya, having eaten and washed off in the icy field shower the sour stench of another's fear and the work of torture. As they left the base, they saw relatives waiting at the gate, most often women like that, rushing up to each vehicle, ready to lie down under a truck, just to learn the truth, to get back a man dead or alive.

Shershnev knew that there was a large diaspora here, many political refugees. But just here and now—the woman should not have been here. Shershnev was not afraid, he did not panic, but he sensed he was being sucked down into a vortex. A woman, just a woman, an ordinary refugee, there were thousands of them here. Pure statistics. Then why the feeling that this was a mean trick, someone's game, a setup from an unknown opponent?

The woman turned around and headed straight for him. Instant relief: no, he did not remember her face.

Then his heart skipped a beat.

The people sitting near the food cart had blocked the lower part of her body. He had thought she was using a walker. They were the handles of a wheelchair.

What Shershnev and Evstifeyev had done to the boy back then left him an adolescent forever. It was only in his face that there was the promise of proud male beauty. Shershnev recognized him. He would have recognized him if he had been wearing makeup, for he had spent a long night in the interrogation container waiting, looking for signs of weakness and emotional fissures in that face. His twin brother? A corpse? Was she wheeling a doll, a wax dummy? Had he lost his mind? It couldn't be! The boy had died, he was dead!

Shershnev understood.

The bastard Mishustin. He had deceived him. Tricked him, the viper. He had promised to finish him off, but instead he secretly sold him to his family. Then Mishustin was killed. Perhaps by the very same purchasers.

They had not worn masks in the container. It was sweaty, hot, and what for, if there would be no witnesses left. The war would continue for a long time and it would hide all traces.

Shershnev thought the whole world was looking at his face. His skin burned without turning red, as if it had been scorched by an icy flame. He recalled the boy's naked body, covered in bruises; the strange, thrilling contrast between the flesh, wet with sweat and blood, and the dry rubber of the gas mask stuck to the head, turning it into a faceless scarecrow. He wanted to be wearing a gas mask, or a carnival disguise, the stupid getup of the guy handing out leaflets in a lion costume; bandages, a lady's dark veil, anything that would hide his face.

Police. They got out of their car and lit up smokes. They looked around, apparently casually but attentively. A fresh team, or they had gotten an urgent bulletin.

The boy was looking a bit past Shershnev. If he moved, the boy would notice him.

Shershnev looked down slowly, rummaged in his pockets as if looking for a wallet or a pack of cigarettes. The wheelchair was coming closer, the policemen had seen it and watched it go.

If the boy recognized him and screamed, he wouldn't get out of there without a fight. Or he could try blindman's bluff, it might work.

Coincidences like this don't happen. It can't be. Foolishness, failure. Why didn't he tell them right away who he was? Why? He'd be alive now. But he was dead! Can't be deader than that! Like the ones in the village Whatever-It's-Called. Naked men stand in the plowed field stand in the snow the first snow is falling hairy men let them stand evening is falling racers firing beyond the village old man in a fur hat funny naked men lie in the plowed field he fell but the hat sticks to his head what fool plowed a field what was he hoping for there's a war on what would grow he wants to knock the hat off his head is it glued on what's holding it the helicopter is whirring creating drifting snow a wolf on the banner white flag pole silver pioneer bugle pain fell off peeling urine-soaked mattresses torn sheets chocolate in the nightstand mother brought it two more weeks to go called his son Maxim like the machine gun she didn't get the joke Maxim Maxim there on the floor blood on his chest who killed him firing pin clicks magazine is empty—

The boy went past, two feet away. His eye was caught by the shop window, gold watches in satin boxes.

The wheelchair was expensive, his clothing modest. Look at him staring at the Rolexes—Shershnev was gabbling to himself—a real mountain dweller, loves gold, it's in their blood, bling and guns.

His self-control had almost returned completely. He could see that the boy would not look back, the woman was taking him away, the police were taking their final drags. Another second or two, and they would all be gone. Good thing Grebenyuk had Neophyte. Fewer unnecessary thoughts. The boy would vanish on his own and never return.

Shershnev didn't give a damn that he was alive. Who cared now anyway? God? Was it God's will to have this ridiculous show?

Behind the bravado, its thin vibrating curtain, lay another thought: How did the boy survive? Mishustin had sold a semi-carcass. Truly: a living corpse. Who had hidden him, nursed him in a place where there was no cover, no food, no medicine, no doctors? Who, how? Half-dead, with squashed fingers and broken ribs—how had he avoided all the traps, roadblocks, minefields, raids? Any soldier who saw him would think he was a wounded fighter. Any roadblock would have arrested him. Whose will, whose power, whose inhuman luck, whose money got the pup out of the place where no one is saved? Who carried him over the mountain passes past the patrols? How? Without documents, wounded—how? And even if he had documents, with a name like that—how? If not Mishustin, then the war would have finished him off. How? How did he get a passport? Or if he didn't, who smuggled him out, in a train car, a trunk, if he couldn't walk?

Shershnev's experience, his knowledge of the rarity of luck, the price of effort, of the possible and the impossible, all cried out: How? And why? Just so that Shershnev would see him? That they would cross paths in a foreign city? It was a huge operation, if you thought about it, even his service would have trouble carrying it off. Then who did it? The boy didn't recognize him and never would. He won't turn around, won't exact revenge.

Shershnev had a thought and immediately dropped it, ashamed of the smarmy naivete of his thinking.

But it stuck.

There was only one feeling in the world that could combine success, persistence, weakness, hope, fear, calculation, and despair, load them together and turn them into a whole saving gesture of fate.

Only one feeling could create this miracle.

Shershnev, a man of war, one of the blue-collar workers of hell, as his colleagues jokingly called one another, was certain of it.

He wanted to protest, demean it, declare it nonexistent—but his rational mind rose against that, his firm, implacable knowledge of war.

But whose love was it? Watching the back of the woman with the wheelchair pushing the twice-born boy, he tried to break the hassling thought, disprove himself. That fat woman's? There were hundreds like her there. A tribe of ravens. Could every one of them do that? Then why didn't it work? It didn't!

There they were, naked in the snow. Not shivering, too proud. Yesterday shots were fired at the roadblock, coming from the village. Let them stand there and freeze. The commanders will decide what to do with them. The old man put on the fur hat, let him enjoy it, why not respect an elderly person . . . It didn't work! There they lie, shot, and the snow is still melting on their bodies. It didn't work!

Shershnev wanted to scream, to shatter windows, anything at all to cross it all out, to return the boy to wherever he had crawled out from. When they called him to receive instruction, one of the generals asked: Isn't there anyone else? With his list . . . if they capture him, break him . . . Shershnev just stood there, knowing that he was the best, and they would send him no matter what the cautious general thought.

And now he thought with dreary emptiness, why didn't he finish off the prisoner himself? If they got caught, his photo would be in all the papers. The boy would recognize him. The circle would close after all.

Shershnev had his first thought of possible failure. He thought that this incident had thrown him off the hunter's rhythm and tossed him into the ordinary, slow time in which everyone else lived; he realized with fear that it had taken away his ability to be a step ahead of the victim, to pass him; someone tremendous and powerful had synchronized their watches.

Shershnev understood he could not be alone. He called Grebenyuk. He responded quickly; he must have been waiting for the call. Shershnev wanted a woman, wanted to take her painfully, spill his weakness and fear into her—like Marina then. After that tour of duty.

CHAPTER 15

Pastor Travniček was praying. Praying for so many days. He was asking for enlightenment for all who were involved and embroiled; he begged God to lead them from the path of evil.

Earlier, in his long-ago former life, he would have sought a solution from God, direction on how to act. He would have wondered: Should I call the police? Act like a citizen and not a priest? He would wonder: What if he was complicating things unnecessarily? Maybe what was going on was not a matter of faith, church, religion? Of God?

Now that his second life was heading for the sunset, he knew that there was no need to ask for guidance. He was the decision himself. The deed. The key. He would not act, but something would happen through him. He was blind and seeing. Empty and full. Alienated and involved.

Travniček had been watching the man on the hill a long time. *Sine ira et studio.* He did not make inquires. He did not try to call him in for a chat. But he kept the resident of the old house in the field of his wakeful inner attention. His past life had taught him to protect particularly those secrets that are clearly known to you but not out in the open.

They tried to turn him into an informer for so many years! To make him tell what he heard in confessions, to inform on his parishioners, his brethren! They were pressuring him, aware of the hidden features of his character: his perceptiveness, his ability to judge a person from the tiniest details, and they tried to make the argument that they needed his reports because they trusted his judgments and wanted to act justly and honestly. And he had had the shameful thought of playing with them, to deceive them and agree—while in fact reporting false information that could not harm anyone. He rejected those thoughts. But he remembered them and never forgave himself. So now he did not rely on perception. It was enough for Travniček that it was he, and not someone else, who learned what was happening; that meant his experience was needed—with all the extremes, narrowness, dead ends, scars of injury, and knowledge of salvation. But how this experience would come in handy, what would happen and what would not, Travniček did not ask himself. His task was simply to be present, here and now.

To pray about the enlightenment of existence. And to wait.

Travniček could not have said exactly when he first realized something special about the man on the hill. He did not have a clear guess or strong suspicions; those concepts were alien to him now.

Weren't there a lot of dried-up scientists, aging bachelors, who liked solitude and lived on their former ambitions? Travniček could name a few more in the area. Did he feel a dark shadow over the house in the beech forest? No.

His flawless pastoral sense was subdued: the man on the hill seemed to be protected by supernatural barriers; cut off from life, from its currents and impact. Hidden in a capsule a priest could not penetrate. Even one like him.

The pastor had never encountered barriers that were fierce on their own. Such extreme suffocating insularity of the spirit, as if a man afraid of living had moved into a coffin.

That is why Travniček knew that the proximity was not accidental; he was there as a sentry, on guard duty. In other places, others guard. But he was given this destiny, this door.

He would do it right, Lord.

Travniček knew that few people took him seriously. In part, he was happy for the mask placed on his face. The ugly muzzle helped to hide his inner tragedy. But now the pastor sensed that the forces of fate had come into play; he would have to reveal his real face.

He was sent—or exiled—to these parts decades ago. From the start, long before his meeting with the man on the hill, he did not seek meaning: Why here? He knew that he was paternally punished by the simplicity of daily life.

"I know thy works, that thou art neither cold nor hot: I would thou wert cold or hot. So then because thou art lukewarm, and neither cold nor hot, I will spew thee out of my mouth." Travniček repeated the familiar and yet unfamiliar words from Revelation, each time unfading and new in the truth directed at him.

But there had been another truth in his past as well.

For the apostle had said: "And these signs shall follow them that believe; In my name shall they cast out devils; they shall speak with new tongues; they shall take up serpents; and if they drink any deadly thing, it shall not hurt them." Travniček not only knew these words by heart, he had experienced them in spirit and flesh; and he re-experienced it, saying the words.

Words about miracles.

With the idea of miracles, he came to the church as a youth. It was many years later he realized that in fact he feared miracles. Feared God, feared the truth of revelation, preferring the God of sacred books, the God of churches and scripture, the God of saints—true but mediated, interpreted, explained, elucidated, expounded. His faith was the faith of culture, artifacts, tradition.

Acutely sensing evil, able to recognize it, he ran to the church from evil, hoping to find salvation in righteousness. But ritual, literal righteousness became something like insurance, a guarantee that God would notice him and forgive his weakness, his fear, and protect him from encountering evil face-to-face.

How long ago that was!

He remembered the early postwar years. Brief years of confusion and hope, when it still seemed that the new civil authorities would restrict the church but not destroy it. Talk of points of conversion. The rejection of open conflict. Of humanistic analogies with Communism.

How quickly that had ended!

When the real persecution began, when youth organizations were branded illegal and criminal, when church meetings were disbanded, when provocateurs were sent in—he had naively hoped that this would lead to a renewal, a rebirth, a return to the heights of faith that had existed during the Roman persecution. He thought it was time for the church to separate itself from the state; to give up that shameful semidependence, full of compromises, that had existed under the Nazis. If the authorities force it to break with them, all the better.

Dreamer!

Alas, he did not understand in time that a path of other compromises was beginning. He could not flee to the West, he could not abandon his flock, even though he often thought that people today would be better off with another priest, more sensitive, gentler, earthly, and understanding. "We are the church of the weak, and we must go to the weak, to the doubters." A celebrated pastor was supposed to have said that.

He turned out to be firm of heart. Another seed grew out of his weakness, the seed of resistance, which made him wonder if it were too human. Did it have any connection to faith? To biblical truths? "Submit yourselves therefore to God. Resist the devil, and he will flee from you," he read the words of the epistle. He asked himself: Are you interpreting it correctly? Isn't it a lie to identify civil authority with the devil's evil? He could not find a clear answer.

He kept feeling something he could not name. Thirst? Longing? Dissatisfaction? *Sehnsucht*, a passionate yearning for saintliness?

That lasted for years. He was moved by the energy of dissatisfaction, a feeling of crowding. He began distributing underground Christian literature, *samizdat*, as they called it in the East. Writing articles under a pseudonym. Collecting money from trusted parishioners to help the persecuted.

Then people from the gray building noticed him. The ones who are supposed to notice. He accepted their approach, their surveillance with anxious joy. It seemed to be a sign that he was acting the right way. Of course, his longing never found either incarnation or release.

How many years he had lived with them, in their shadow! Irredeemable, irreplaceable years! Slow years, like the ripening of juniper berries in the churchyard.

He grew accustomed to them. To the surveillance from nearby houses. To the cars that followed him on the empty highways at night. To strangers who deftly tried to worm their way into his trust. To secret searches of house and church, the feeling that nasty fingers had touched his things. To ears eavesdropping on his telephone conversations. To eyes reading his mail and following him on the street. To marked letters. To denunciatory articles in the newspapers. To faked "demands" to replace him with a pastor who would be more attentive to the parishioners' needs. To petty and consequential nastiness.

He prayed for those who persecuted and tormented him. He developed an acute, borrowed sense of deceit, surveillance, bugs, dangerous, ambivalent things offered as gifts or appearing accidently. He tried to live in knowledge but without the poison of suspicion; the latter was rational but meaningless, for within it lay the victory of evil; to be not blind yet not unnecessarily seeing in the whirlpool, the circle dance of faces, any of which could be false.

He became inconvenient. For some in the hierarchy as well. He was transferred—away from big cities to modest village parishes; there was both care and concern that he was becoming too visible, too irritating to the authorities. Some of his fellow pastors said that he was led by the sin of ambition, sought personal glory rather than the good of the Church.

But he was led by his yearning, his will to sainthood that found no outlet.

Evil was approaching, palpating, testing. Three times women tried to seduce him: one, he was certain, of her own free will, but the other two . . . When they dispatched him to the sticks, he bought a car. Friends helped. But soon he lost his driver's license; he was stopped on the road, they did a blood test, alleged he was driving while drunk. You managed to repeat Christ's miracle, he said at that trial, turning water into wine. He bought a moped, it didn't require a license. The moped was stolen. He knew that one day they would deal with him seriously. He even desired it—not petty attacks, adolescent pranks, but true martyrdom, the redemptive crown of thorns. People gathered around him, people who expected something from him, seeing him as a man who had the right to speak.

But when God appeared to him and said the Word, he was not prepared. He did not understand. He did not accept. He did not recognize. He rejected Him because in his pride he thought he knew how He would act. He thought he would recognize His will and would not allow secular voices to lead him into error.

He was blind!

Now when his life was almost at the end, he had become neither bishop nor preacher. He had not cultivated his original talents, and the borrowed ones were taken away. The Lord crushed his pride and gave him faith. That was why he could focus on the daily affairs of the church: roof repairs, balancing the books, registering births and deaths.

He thrived in unexpecting expectation.

He had been tried and set aside; now the time had come.

Events were set into motion, the masks were about to fall, the protective seals would vanish. Travniček understood that the man on the hill could cost him dearly; people like him were very expensive goods. They had hidden him, given him shelter and money; that meant that there were others willing to do so. Other people might have fears and temptations, responsibilities, rules, orders. So he would take his man upon himself. No matter what lay hidden in the locked vessel of another's soul.

He was the only one who could do this safely for everyone.

Travniček started praying—for enlightenment for the man on the hill; for those who did evil and were now persecuted; for the hounds, the people with dead hearts.

For the gift of the incomprehensible.

CHAPTER 16

Usually, if he could not sleep, Kalitin listed the formulas of the substances that failed testing. They were never again synthesized; they vanished from the world, remaining only in lab notes; their names led to emptiness, to nonexistence.

But the time for long portions of dreams had ended. The clever god Hypnos had left the house and his sleepless brother stood at the door, refusing gifts.

Kalitin felt alone facing death and memory. He remembered almost everything he liked to remember and much of what he hoped to forget. He was ready to stop and fall asleep. But memory—unwanted, rejected—had come to exact a penalty for its long incarceration.

Kalitin got out of bed, fanned the flames, added kindling. Yesterday the eastern sky would have been getting light over the ridge by now. But today brought heavy clouds and rain beyond the mountains, hiding the dawn.

He needed just a few hours of sleep. And then he would leave. Had he been invited to join the investigation? Yes. So he would go away. The decision about where came on its own. The shore of the Arabian Sea. To a country run by the army and intelligence service; they would have a real appreciation for Neophyte and its creator.

Kalitin didn't bother to search for the embassy address online. He had walked past it once, he had a vague recollection of the building, recognizably faceless. He wondered if it was under surveillance. Probably. A permanent post in some nearby apartment. Cameras with face recognition. Well, the main thing was to hand over his letter. The embassy people would find him. He would buy a new SIM card at a street kiosk. He'd have to leave all his things behind. Like the last time. In his new life, everything would be new.

The only things from the past would be Neophyte and himself.

Neophyte. When Kalitin finally had a full-fledged laboratory again, it could be moved from its travel container into a stationary vessel. He would be able to see how it was affected by the passage of time. That was the main enemy of all preparations of its class, hyperactive but not very stable. So it was a question— was it Neophyte in the container? Or just Mr. Fizz, bubbly water, no more harmful than children's shampoo? That thought caused Kalitin pain. He couldn't even imagine the death of Neophyte. Substance. Being. A cherished being.

Vera had wanted a child. A son. She must have known that he could have only one child: one born in a test tube. He sensed that children would not be given to him. He saw it as a kind of scientist's blessing. But Vera . . .

Kalitin had blamed himself so many times for the marriage, planned to get a divorce. But he knew too well why he had married. For the same reason he had joined the Party, had gone to rallies and *subbotnik* volunteer activities.

The Island protected you, but it demanded loyalty. Beyond its borders lay the terrarium of science, where predatory monsters of various eras lived, as if in a crazy garden of time.

Elders. Abettors of the bloody destruction of scientific schools that culminated in execution and exile. Collaborators in murders executed with the help of critical articles. Connoisseurs of fatal polemics in the scholarly argot poisoned by Marxism, rivals for the attention of Stalin, the Giant of All Sciences. Creators of false doctrines born of ideological dogmas that destroyed, like decay, entire branches of knowledge.

Kalitin had met them in the hallways of institutes and ministries—the influential gray undead, who extended their time thanks to former privileges, medicines, hospitals, mineral spas, massages, and transplants. They were still deadly and could still devour you—if not alive, as before—if a new theory disproved their work of forty years ago, for which they had received bonuses, orders, and the title academician.

Youngsters. Shrewd Party activists, who did not write their own dissertations, scions of prominent families set up in science. These sleek creatures were as bloodthirsty as the old men, even though they did not have fangs and claws: the breed had degenerated. But they knew how to spread rumors, start an intrigue, pilfer a topic, steal an idea, become a coauthor, cut off financing.

On the Island, close to Zakharyevsky, Kalitin was practically invulnerable. But on the Island, the substances were only born. They had to be promoted, brought out into the world, albeit a secret one, and there Kalitin was, and therefore the products were, in danger.

Kalitin knew the strong and weak points in his CV, his tested and retested biography. When Zakharyevsky gave him the friendly advice to start a family because it would help his candidacy advance through the Party bureaucracy, Kalitin already knew his choice.

Vera.

Forgotten name.

Once he and Vera watched an episode of *Animal World*. It was about iguana fry spawned on the beach: thousands are born, many hundreds die, dozens reach the water, three or four survive, one will live to sexual maturity.

That was when Kalitin was seriously thinking about the idea for Neophyte. It was like seeing a reflection of his own thoughts: thousands of neophytes, nameless numbered substances born in test tubes; most will be useless, dozens will show some capability but will have flaws that override it; only two or three will get indexed and early names; they will fight the real battle for life, for realization, for a place in the registers and production plans.

There will be only one Neophyte with a capital N.

He felt his loneliness acutely, the useless burden of their marriage: Was Vera capable of sharing that? Understanding that he was also a neophyte, one of the few who thirsted for fulfillment more than anything?

Vera, whose name meant faith. He could say the word without meaning her.

It turned out that there was meaning in their marriage. She had saved him. And given him a discovery.

He was required to run the test with Neophyte's first, experimental version. Predecessors of the substance. He was unhappy with it, he imagined that a mistake had crept into the calculations and the mixture was not strong enough.

Vera volunteered. She was qualified to do it.

A crack in the valve they'd overlooked. The valve exploded, a metal shard broke the plastic box and the super reliable protective gear. The exhaust ventilation worked well, only a minuscule amount got inside the clothing. Just a few molecules, you could say. But it was Neophyte, the real Neophyte. Kalitin had correctly guessed the base composition.

Neophyte had killed Vera instantly.

It was the first thing it did.

It took payment for its birth.

Neophyte was exactly what Kalitin had dreamed.

Not just a substance.

It was that, and not his wife's death, that stunned Kalitin. He could not admit that he was afraid.

Frightened not as a chemist whose substance turned out to be devilishly effective. But as a creator, whose creation, intended to be a faithful servant or loyal soldier, came to life beyond measure, escaping obedience, insubordinate to its creator.

Neophyte was too fierce. It should have been forgotten, written off as a failure, the way they put down mad dogs of fighting breeds that cannot be trained.

But Kalitin could not give it up.

He had put everything into it; he knew he would not have a second enlightenment.

Neophyte was so secret that Vera's body could not be sent to the hospital morgue. Neophyte had touched her and she became a vessel for the secret.

The autopsy showed there were no traces of the substance. Kalitin's hypothesis was confirmed. Neophyte was untraceable.

They expressed condolences, gave him leave, wanted to send him to a sanatorium in the south. He said he wanted to return to work. It would be easier for him there. For Vera's sake.

They allowed it.

He began his attempts to tame his creation, solve the problems of preservation, stability—without that he could not hope for certification, for its production.

But Neophyte turned out to be excessively sensitive and high-spirited. If he changed the original composition just an iota, the whole became unbalanced. Neophyte was born to be just as it was; limited in use because of its wildness, its instant passion to kill.

For years, Kalitin struggled for minute improvement; he was close to the success he begged from fate. But the country fell apart, the Island collapsed, and Neophyte was not born officially, remaining nonexistent, unrecorded, as if its name doomed it to perpetual beginner status.

Neophyte.

Kalitin had proposed the name long ago. He hated ciphers that meant nothing. They seemed to steal something from the substance, something that appears when a thing has the right name, a pet with the perfect diminutive, a secret of the soul, a drawing of fate.

He went through dozens of names, checked dictionaries— none of them worked.

One day Kalitin took a walk on the edge of the testing ground. There was a ravine overgrown with angelica, a stream pouring from the slimy stone wall. Beyond the ravine were broken, tumbledown tombstones of an abandoned cemetery; the wooden village houses had rotted long ago, but the limestone slabs stuck out through last year's flattened grass. There, at the ravine, Kalitin came up with clever, elegant, lively name: Neophyte, as if someone had placed it on his tongue.

There was no substance yet, no formula, no path to it—only his brazen idea.

He had joined Zakharyevsky's laboratory not knowing that he would be working on chemical weapons. He had signed a nondisclosure agreement before he had anything to disclose.

Of course, the institute had other areas of work. He learned about them only later, after receiving his first independent assignment from Zakharyevsky.

Kalitin did not regret a thing. The ontology of death that he encountered as a researcher set before him scientific questions of incredible scope and depth.

Now he could admit that he had never been an atheist in the strict sense of the word. But he was not a believer, either. He knew that there was a higher power in the world. He knew it as a practitioner who had experienced epiphanies that could not be explained rationally. A prospector, a miner, depending on these insights, knowing how to find the intuitive path.

He did not ascribe them to God or the devil, to human nature or the qualities of knowledge.

Probably, deep inside, he thought himself an archaic creature, a shaman traveling through other worlds in the search of sources, artifacts of power. It was no accident that he was a collector; they did a lot of digging in the test field, and those were areas of ancient nomads, ancient stops along the river, and the land always yielded up gifts—ancient, original symbols of sacred, clumsy Paleolithic figures, and also flint axes and arrowheads.

Kalitin believed that he was a creator alongside other creators, since he did not draw water from some black well, did not find inspiration in blood and suffering. Huge eagles often circled above the Island; Kalitin liked the birds, liked the winds, the unrestrained sunsets, the wild expanses. It was from them that he drew vision, inspiration, the sense of the significance of his own life. This fact was proof to him that he was like all the other talents; divisions were hypocritical. Anyone who condemned him simply did not know that the same wind and sunsets ran in his blood as in that of any other gifted person; Neophyte was as much a product of inspiration, risk, and art as was the Winged Victory of Samothrace, as Mendeleev's table of elements.

Kalitin remembered and could relive the first flash of understanding, the guiding meteor.

He was working on Zakharyevsky's orders with vegetable substances, stable, acting instantly, but leaving traces just as stable. He tried to lower their visibility, blurring, dissolving, turning them into a transparent veil.

But the stubborn substance would not yield, and Kalitin, furious, threw his pencil on the floor and stared at the lab ceiling, a cupola of the former church, with exhaust vents hanging down. Only one angel in the corner, cut off at the chest, remained of the original painting. Anywhere else it would have been painted over, but the Party committee was not allowed inside the lab. Kalitin liked looking at the thoughtful face in a gold wreath, at the narrow golden tube pressed to the angelic lips. The angel was in Kalitin's power, a ghost of another era, herald of a trial that did not take place, having outlived the prerevolutionary world in which his image had sense, the direct power of significance.

While gazing at that angel with the special stubbornness of the last shard that does not wish to vanish, steadfastly witnessing the existence of the whole, Kalitin realized that death by its very nature is a dirty thing, and that was not a metaphor. Death always left clues, the multifaceted natural traces that the wise investigator will understand; that is how the world is made, those are its laws.

To bypass, trick those laws, to make death come unseen, penetrating every cover and leaving no trace is the highest power, the ability to directly rule existence.

At that moment Kalitin—who was still young—vacillated.

He understood that the appearance of death, its eternal fate to leave traces, be known, is a natural good, the red signal thread sewn and woven into the fabric of the world. The original law of retribution is encoded and realized in matter. That means the possibility of executing it. The possibility of the existence of the concepts of crime, guilt, revenge, retribution, repentance. Morality per se.

Kalitin hesitated but he was not frightened. He had touched a certain border—the sensation was clear, real. He wanted to step beyond it.

When Kalitin created Neophyte, he saw that it was impossible to bypass the protective mechanism. The law was more complicated than he thought.

Neophyte was weak because of its strength. It left no trace and was lethal, but too unstable as a chemical; the absolute of two qualities to the detriment of all others. Too lethal and there-fore not viable.

Neophyte could not be directed, untraceable but dependent on the container. The experts had immediate questions on the tactics of use: How to deploy a substance that kills the killer as well as the victim? They came up with the lame scheme of leaving the target alone with the Neophyte and then removing the ves-sel, the container; that's how they killed the banker. The scheme worked, but it removed Neophyte's main advantage: secrecy.

Back then, at the start of the journey, before Neophyte was formulated as a clear concept, Kalitin was filled with hope.

He became a fan of death. He studied how people died, how that took place chemically and physiologically. He listened to talks by invited specialists, doctors who thought they were entrusting their knowledge to a chemist working on a secret medicine for the Central Committee. At the City morgue he learned from the forensic experts. He read histories of epidemics and researched the death of all living things: plants, mushrooms, insects, plank-ton, ecosystems.

The first, the simplest, path of experiments he chose led to the creation of a twin substance.

He had long thought that all substances with their various fighting temperaments, duration of action, vulnerabilities, and strong points had twins in the human world. Among people you can call yourself something else, random, unassociated—and so Kalitin created dark twins for substances for civilian use, achieved identical traces that no one could interpret as evidence of murder.

But that was still only a partial, imperfect solution. The trace remained, and in unfortunate circumstances could raise suspicions.

Once Kalitin went night fishing with the chief of security, Zakharyevsky's old friend. Called back into the acting reserves, the general respected and nurtured Kalitin in his rough way. But his peasant habits had to be indulged from time to time, for instance, carp fishing. The security chief was of interest to Kalitin, too. Uneducated, hopelessly behind the times, he was a fossil from a bygone era, from the sins, filth, and blood that Kalitin wanted to avoid. The simple and meaningless death by bullet reigned there, indiscriminately taking millions of souls. Kalitin was creating a different death—rational, focused; its morality and justification lay in its singularity. But that was why the general interested Kalitin, he reeked of wild blood; against his background, Kalitin's inner principles stood in stark relief. Besides which, there was a profound and unobvious similarity to their work, which preordained and blessed their alliance, the scientist and the KGB officer. The security chief was a professional whose ethics were expediency; he knew how to open people up and take the shortest path to truth. That's how Kalitin acted in science.

They fished by the light of a kerosene lantern that cast long shadows on the sand. Nothing was biting. The security chief sucked on his stinking Belomor cigarette, stared at length, thoughtless, at the fishing pole's bell, sipped at his flask of alcohol infusion of birch fungus, real turpentine—Kalitin tried it once and almost burned his throat. They had brought three newbies to the Island, recent graduates of the special school, as he had once been. Kalitin was looking for an opportunity to ask informally about one he was planning to take on as a lab assistant.

"I wouldn't," the old man said in a friendly tone, instantly understanding why Kalitin was interested. "He's a fool. Talks too much. If he keeps blabbing we'll take away his access."

"What does he blab about?" Kalitin asked neutrally.

"Ghosts," the old man answered slowly. "Those, damn it, specters. Seen them in the cellar."

"That's nonsense," Kalitin exclaimed sincerely.

"Nonsense, but not nonsense," he said in a lecturing tone. "We're in a special place. With history. Events took place here in the olden days. Shouldn't gab in that direction."

Kalitin felt the old man was talking about something personal, long past. He knew some details of his biography. Zakharyevsky had enlightened him, explaining how to deal with the general.

Kalitin wondered more than once as he thought about the old man: Why didn't they just round people up, shoot and bury them? Why did they have investigations, write documents, observe the formalities, if they knew it was all a lie? Why all those procedures? He understood now, looking at the old man: for the sake of the executioners. The procedures served as guardrails, to keep them from going mad and becoming insubordinate.

The old man had fallen silent. Kalitin felt that the topic of ghosts had upset him, the idea that death was reversible, that witnesses could arise out of nowhere. He did not believe in ghosts. But it was pleasant observing the superstitious, childish fears of the all-powerful chief of security.

The bell jingled. Deep in the water the carp had taken the bait and pulled it. The old man tugged, then cursed in disappointment. "Gone, the bastard."

Suddenly in the cupola of light from the lantern white flakes swirled like a snow shower. The wind had carried August mayflies from the expanses of the river, wandering creatures of the night that would not live till dawn.

The mayflies threw themselves at the heated glass, striving for the flame, turning to charcoal. The lamp was like a magical vessel calling them out of the darkness.

The mayflies covered the sand, the tideline, like fallen constellations. Kalitin felt piercing delight. He now knew what his Neophyte should be: short-lived, vanishing in the shadows of the world, capable before disintegrating of performing just one wish: death.

Mayflies. Glorious mayflies. The rusty light of the kerosene flame. The living white blizzard at the end of summer, the dance of departure. A foretaste of blizzards to come. The swoon of winter's white sleep.

Kalitin fell asleep, feeling the tremor of light-winged shadows under his shut eyelids.

CHAPTER 17

They started out later than planned. When the manager at the rental place typed in the information on Shershnev-Ivanov's driver's license, the computer crashed. He reloaded and tried again—another crash.

The manager apologized; Shershnev thought, is this a trap? The license had been issued properly and added to the database.

"Let's use mine, what's the difference," Grebenyuk suggested. "Let's try some magic," he added, addressing Shershnev.

The computer worked. They were given a car. V6 turbo, but not flashy, the upgraded version of a popular family sedan. Local production, thousands like it on the road.

Grebenyuk got behind the wheel and when they had traveled a bit he asked, "Are you all right?"

"I'm fine," Shershnev replied.

"It's a strange feeling," Grebenyuk said. "As if someone is slowing us down. The border agents. The train. Now the computer."

Shershnev looked at him with feigned surprise.

"What's up? Didn't get enough sleep?"

"I did. Sorry. Just this stupid idea."

"Happens," Shershnev replied.

He hadn't expected such perception from the tech guy. It had suited him to know nothing much about his partner: what for, they weren't going to be friends. He was told he was a pro, and that was enough. Now Shershnev regretted not feeling him out, learning his background. It was too late now, it would be clumsy. He'd have to wait for the right moment.

Shershnev was glad to get out of the city and roll toward Germany, head for the goal at last, and leave yesterday behind. To convince himself that the boy from the past was just a crazy accident, an unsummoned souvenir of his own history. And now Grebenyuk with his question!

The weather had turned bad, too. Clouds filled the sky, and it was drizzling. Grebenyuk switched on the wipers, pushed the washer button—two weak jets sprayed and fell. They parked, bought water, turned on the GPS. The system loaded and set the course—it seemed right in terms of mileage, a little over three hours, thought dubious Shershnev—and they set off. The female voice gave orders in English: left, right, traffic circle, second exit.

In the end, the disembodied lady led them into a traffic jam on a road under construction. The turn she wanted was blocked.

"They haven't updated the app, I guess," said Grebenyuk, and Shershnev waited to see if he would continue, bring up the strange, silly holdups. But the major said nothing more, and pulled back into traffic.

It was no longer drizzling but pouring. The wipers were on high, the right one squeaking. They got out on the highway, but the cars were barely moving there, either. Far on the hill they could see the rhythmic pulse of blue lights.

Minus ninety minutes.

At last they reached the scene of the accident. Police were letting cars drive against traffic. An overturned truck lay across the road. The asphalt was covered in scraps of wooden crates and shards of bottles. Dark wine puddles grew lighter in the rain, and a sour smell wafted in the opened window. On the side of the road, emergency workers huddled around a crushed car. The soggy air bags were covered in blood.

"Good thing they had some wine," Grebenyuk joked. "There's enough for the wake."

He had changed gears once in the driver's seat—a real technician. He drove wisely, efficiently, and Shershnev felt the superiority he acquired from the car, its 240 horsepower that recognized a steady hand.

Minus two and half hours.

"Stop looking at the time. We'll get there," Grebenyuk said confidently.

He shifted to sports mode, and then raced down the left lane. The road was clear after the traffic jam, the rain was coming down even harder, the wipers were barely adequate. Grebenyuk drove steadily, without slowing down for curves. Shershnev was filled with confidence, watching the wind-flattened fabric covers of trucks, trees, mileposts flash by.

A red car ahead, an undersized city vehicle. Grebenyuk flashed his lights. He wouldn't let them pass, perhaps ready for a left exit. Grebenyuk began passing on the right, the road curved, when the red car also moved to the right without signaling.

They passed, just avoiding a skid, scraping the curb.

A dog in the backseat. A Giant Schnauzer. The windows were fogged inside, and the driver couldn't see a thing.

Three and half hours.

They should have been approaching the site of the operation and checking it out. It would be dark soon, especially in this weather.

"In ten kilometers turn right," the navigator announced.

Shershnev tensed. "That's too soon."

"We'll see when we get there," Grebenyuk replied. "But I think it is too soon."

They reached the top of the hill and through the blurred corridor of slanting rain they saw the dark foothills enveloped in blue-gray fog.

The car pulled off the road.

It sounded like a shot with a silencer.

Grebenyuk held the wheel. The right front tire had blown out, the rubber flapped on the road. They stopped right at the barrier; below was a steep boulder-filled slope.

When they removed the tire, they found a shard of bottle glass.

"This is unbelievable," Grebenyuk shook his head. "Maybe we shouldn't have spent time with broads last night. You know, they can do anything they want if they don't like you. We should have tipped them."

Shershnev couldn't tell if his partner was joking. He just couldn't wait for it all to end. The target would die, the bad luck would end. They just had to get to him.

Good thing the spare tire was full-sized, even though the jack was kind of puny. They got dirty changing the tire, and they needed to get to a store and buy some jeans; his other pair, that is, Ivanov's, were left behind in the suitcase lost at the airport.

"I had something like this happen once," Grebenyuk continued. "Smile, you're on candid camera. It was on an assignment. I realized the trick was not to worry, struggle, or panic. Like a swamp or quicksand if you're drowning. It will let you go."

"Got it," said Shershnev. "Let's go."

They were approaching a fork in the road. The GPS was indicating for them to go right: a turn in three kilometers, one kilometer, five hundred meters. Shershnev used the touchscreen to zoom in on the map. The electronic assistant was sending them on a side road through the next valley for some reason.

"Well, are we turning?" Grebenyuk asked.

"Straight," Shershnev ordered.

Up ahead, two highways merged. On the broad curving ramp, Shershnev noticed that they had caught up with the red car. It had its emergency blinkers on: the driver must have gotten lost and was looking for his exit. Grebenyuk slowed down and moved left. But the little red car suddenly jumped in reverse. Grebenyuk braked and went into reverse, but the red car still hit their fender.

They both jumped out. A dent, paint scraped off. Nothing terrible. But now their car was too noticeable.

The red car's bumper and rear light were smashed.

Grebenyuk suddenly laughed and banged his fist on the hood. "Fuck. Were you waiting to ambush us, you asshole?"

Shershnev relaxed. This was a comedy. A joke. When I tell this story later, no one will believe me. This guy obviously had lunch while we were changing the tire. And pulled out just as we came by, a kamikaze asshole.

"Should we get out of here?" Grebenyuk offered.

"What if he calls the police? Says it's our fault. Rear-ended him. And gives them a whole story, that we tried to make him swerve and caused the accident."

The driver got out, a fat, gray-haired man in glasses. He had been calming the frightened, barking dog. He didn't look bewildered, however; he bent over his trunk, looked under it, and said something in the local language. Shershnev indicated that he did not understand and replied in English—uselessly, since the man continued yapping in his own tongue. He took out a phone, called someone, gabbled, and then signaled with his palm to wait, and got back in his car.

The merriment faded. Shershnev and Grebenyuk looked at each other. The rain had stopped, the last drops banging on the windshield.

"We have to wait. We'll bullshit our way out of it," said Shershnev.

He was seething inside. The laughter was replaced almost instantly by fury, to which he could not succumb; but he couldn't suppress it either, only postpone it, and Shershnev promised himself, soon, soon you will be able to feel it.

The police came about twenty minutes later; it felt like an hour. They exchanged a few words with the driver of the red car and came over to them.

"He was backing up on the highway. It's not our fault," Shershnev began in English.

"Yes, yes, we know," the policeman responded with some surprise at his aggressiveness. "The driver at fault reported it. He called us to write up a report for the rental company."

Grebenyuk winked.

The report was written quickly. They took a few photos of the damaged fender with their iPhones. The officer, a young provincial cop with good school English, asked as he returned their documents in a bored manner, looking for something to distract him from work, "Where are you headed?"

They had the rehearsed reply to fit their cover. There were no usual tourist sites near the subject's residence, no castles, thermal springs, or canyons with observation platforms. There was only one spot. The embassy people went there every year to lay wreaths. So they proposed it.

"The museum," said Shershnev. "You know, the memorial . . ."

"You've passed it," said the cop with animation. "We can show you the road, we're headed in that direction anyway."

Shershnev didn't risk telling him that they've already been there—what if the driver had told them they had already met on the road? The odometer would not match their mileage. He was at a loss for an answer, trapped by the excessive amiability, idiotic readiness to help. One cretin called the police to take care of them. Other cretins were now going to accompany them. Why didn't they just leave them alone? And what made him say that? He could have avoided an answer. Everything seemed fine, but words are like instant glue, holding so that you can't tear away.

"Thank you," Shershnev said. "We'd be grateful."

"What's the matter with you?" Grebenyuk whispered in the car. "What the fuck do we need this for?"

"How could I refuse?" Shershnev answered in irritation, angered by his mistake. "Say, oh, we changed our mind? Let's go back? We can't be memorable. We have to behave the way they expect. I remember the map. It's not far. We'll zip over and back. Quick trip."

"They're hard to understand," Grebenyuk insisted. "Can you imagine our cops behaving this way?"

"This is Europe," Shershnev said. "Get used to it."

CHAPTER 18

Kalitin awoke long past noon. His head was clear, even though he had drunk over half a bottle of cognac. In the shower, he decided to leave tomorrow, not today. Clean out the computer, burn some papers in the evening. Make very sure that the container of Neophyte was ready for the trip, and could withstand bouncing on the road, unexpected falls, jolts, or bangs.

The perfume bottle had been kept for decades in the safe. Kalitin, deprived of a laboratory, could not move Neophyte into a more reliable vessel. He couldn't even check the container: Was the valve intact? The technicians on the Island had promised that the loaded bottle would remain hermetically sealed forever. But Kalitin remembered his wife's fate and was extra careful.

The refrigerator was empty, and he had not been in the mood for food on the way home yesterday. He decided to have lunch in the village. An omelet with sausage and cracklings, invigorating tea with ginger. Then home and a nap for a couple of hours, followed by a hot and cold shower. Coffee. That would take away the feebleness in his fingers, sharpen his mind, and he could carefully pack Neophyte, that capricious and dangerous child, into the transportation box.

He drove the usual way past the church and turned toward the river. The restaurant was empty, people here kept country hours for meals. Kalitin went to the far terrace over the deep waters of the mill, where silvery trout stayed in the slow circling water, catching flies and bugs from the surface. They knew him here, and made the omelet the way he liked it—without over-cooking the bacon, adding sweet peppers, and he was sorry he would have to leave all this.

Behind him came professionally polite steps: must be the landlady. She often brought him something on the house, strudel or crepes with jam.

But it was Travniček. Black cassock, expressionless face. Kalitin shuddered.

"Forgive me," said that pastor. "Good morning. May I speak with you?"

It must be the roof or stained glass windows again, Kalitin thought with regret. When it came to repairs, Travniček was unbearable. "Why do you get so upset," someone said to him once. "The church has been here six hundred years and will be there six hundred more."

"It is God's House," Travniček replied loftily, as if he really thought that God lived in that stone barn.

"Of course. Would you like some tea?" Kalitin decided to have some fun before leaving and maybe even give him money, let the ridiculous priest enjoy an unexpected victory.

"Thank you." The pastor sat down, adjusting his cassock with a fussy, feminine gesture. "You drove past yesterday, I waved to you, but you did not stop."

It's starting, Kalitin thought. What broke or leaked this time?

"I was just about to go to your place, but here you are. That's a good sign."

Something new, Kalitin told himself. The extortionist never went door-to-door before.

"You see, while you were away . . . People came to your house. Agents. External surveillance."

"Agents? To my house?" Kalitin did not quite understand what he had said.

He looked at the awkward pastor, his plump hands with infrequent colorless hairs, his flabby breasts—must be hormonal, he thought—beneath the cassock. A miracle of nature!

"Yes. To you," the pastor replied simply.

"Pastor, you imagined it." Kalitin spoke sincerely. "What agents? What am I, a spy? Must have been some tourists who got lost. You've been watching too much television."

But inside, it was as if a glass rod used in mixing reagents had snapped.

"You haven't asked whom I saw," Travniček said with a small smile. "Fine. I won't insist. But I will explain for your own good why I cannot make a mistake. I don't like talking about it, but . . . I spent nineteen years under surveillance. In the country that no longer exists, thank God. Every day. In church. On the street. In the store. I know their breed all too well. Looks. Manners. Methods. So, they were agents. People from my past. However, this time with Slavic faces."

Kalitin could hear the water rushing in the stones. The pastor's sentences were dissolving, lost behind the roar that had grown suddenly and threateningly.

The house. The container with Neophyte. The unfinished

omelet on his plate. The plans for tomorrow—it all fell away. Now there was only his body, aged, weak, so easily shot with a bullet.

No, no, there would be no bullet, Kalitin thought in impotent horror. They would send someone with Neophyte. That would be like them.

The very thought that Neophyte was somewhere nearby, in someone else's hands, made Kalitin dizzy. He remembered Vera's blue, inhuman face. Why hadn't he destroyed all the other samples before he defected? He had been in the lab. He couldn't do it. He was sorry.

"How long ago?" Kalitin asked, controlling himself. He hoped it was yesterday or the day before, which meant he had plenty of time.

"Nine days ago," Travniček replied. "Alas. I didn't know where to call you. I think they reported that no one had seen them. It's amazing but people often don't notice priests. We are an anachronism for them. Do you have a place to go?"

"Why do you ask?" Kalitin asked automatically; nine days took away almost all his hope.

"You live here. You are my parishioner, even if you don't go to church," Travniček replied with dignity.

The pastor's words engendered a strange sense of trust, as if he had been sent a smart animal who would save him, a clever lizard that knew the secret passages in the rocks.

His mind began calculating possibilities.

He was found after the invitation to join the investigation. That means the leak was from there. He couldn't ask for help, it might go to a mole. That may even be the plan: make him jumpy, ask for help, for evacuation.

How many would come? Two. Kalitin had consulted the people who wrote the manual. They would come by car. It was very likely that they were already here. Near the house. In the woods. In the hills. With binoculars. Waiting for him to come back.

There was nowhere to run. No one to ask for help. He had to get into the house. Neophyte was there, his ticket. Without the deadly substance and with a fatal diagnosis no one needed him. Just garbage. They would not treat his disease until he first showed them his wares.

"Let's get your car out of the parking lot," Travniček said gently. "They certainly know your license plate number. I assume you don't want to call the police?"

Kalitin shook his head.

"Let's go," Travniček said. "Don't forget to pay your bill."

"Where?" Kalitin asked, getting up and reaching for his wallet.

"To the church. Where else?" Travniček replied. "You don't think they'll look for you in the church?"

Kalitin had no answer.

"Why are you helping me?" he demanded as soon as the stepped over the threshold of the church. The car was hidden behind shrubs in the area for garbage cans; if you didn't know it was there, you wouldn't find it.

"It's my duty," the priest said, locking the door.

"All right. I'll ask a different way. Why are you helping—me?" Kalitin was overcome with hysterical laughter, a response to the fear.

"It's my duty," Travniček repeated.

"Listen, you don't know about me," Kalitin giggled. "I'm not calling the police. Doesn't that worry you?"

"Wait, I'll bring some wine," Travniček responded kindly. "It's for communion," adding apologetically. "But you need a sip or two. To calm down."

Kalitin remained standing in confusion.

It was the first time he had entered the church that he had seen from the outside a thousand times.

The vaulted ceiling reminded Kalitin of his laboratory. Yes. They had worked in a former church. The same narrow windows, extremely thick walls, the same design.

He looked closely at the walls, slowly walked along the rows of benches of hard wood. It was dark. He couldn't see well. However, the paintings would have been flat and meaningless to him even in good light. Who were the bearded men with haloes—apostles, saints? What were they doing? What was the significance of their positions?

He reached the altar. The vaults were more curved and the figures on them hung above Kalitin. The Last Judgment, that he understood. It was the only thing he could understand in the church without prompting.

He looked again at the architectural composition, the shape of the space. He remembered the trumpeting angel cut at the waist and thought: form dictates subject, happy that the ability to think deeply and nimbly had returned to him.

Below, at eye level, horned devils with blue tongues were attacking sinners with pitchforks; multieyed monsters dragged the bodies into the purple abyss, below floor level.

Above, in the diffuse aureole of light, the heavenly host

conquered creatures that had flown too high, into forbidden territory. In the center, Jesus stood on a cloud. Along the sides, in the wedge shapes of the vaults, angels blew into long trumpets.

The one on the right remotely resembled the one on the Island, as if two artists had painted the same creature.

This would have been there, Kalitin thought, seeing the entire painting. That's what! The Last Judgment! And we were working right under it. Among invisible devils and monsters that had been removed from the walls.

Kalitin shivered. It was cold in the church. The porous limestone seemed to have absorbed the river damp and was now releasing it inside.

Travniček returned with the wine. Kalitin gulped it down—sweet, fragrant.

He decided to stay there until nightfall. Really: Who would look for him in the church?

In the dark, he would go through the woods to the back door. They didn't know that he knew about them; if the killers were there, they would expect him to drive up to the front door. As long as Travniček did not change his mind and turn him in. Should he ask him to go to the house? How would he explain the container?

"I'll help you," Travniček said unexpectedly. "But you must hear me out," he said solemnly and severely.

"All right," Kalitin said carefully. Let him say whatever he wanted, as long as he could remain here until night. Strange, but he felt safe in the church. He pictured how it looked from the outside—grim, dark, belonging to no one, and that inspired confidence similar to what he felt on the Island.

"Just don't take offense," Travniček added. "I'm not good at being a pastor. Do you remember Hessman? The real estate agent who sold you the house?"

"Yes," Kalitin said, confused. "What about him?"

"I'll try to explain," Travniček continued, arms crossed on his chest. "You went to his funeral. Hessman used to be an officer in state security. He worked in the department overseeing religion."

"Did he tell you about me?" Kalitin asked hurriedly, remembering the perceptive agent's deduction about him.

"No, of course not. We rarely talked. I was the only one who knew who he was. Hessman—you know this—turned out to be a very good real estate agent. His dealings were flawless. If he had not joined the service as a youth, he could have lived an honest life. Selling houses. And he committed evil only on instruction. He followed orders, no more than that."

"Why are you telling me this?" Kalitin asked nervously.

"It may seem like I'm beating about the bush. I told you I'm a bad pastor," Travniček said in a hurry. "That Hessman . . . You see, I had run-ins with other people from his department. They approached the work differently."

"How?" Kalitin was amused; let the fool babble while they waited.

"I used to call it creativity in the name of evil," Travniček replied modestly. "Even like this: the problem of creativity in the name of evil."

Kalitin decided to take a dig at the pastor, so free, so serious and naive. He knew that Travniček would not throw him out whatever he said or did. Kalitin thought of the Island and enjoying the fact that Travniček did not know who he was, asked with feigned animation: "What do you know about evil? What have you seen? Do you think that evil is the surveillance you experienced?"

"You are right," Travniček admitted. "I know little. Less than I should. But you are also not right." His voice changed, deeper, calmer. "I have seen evil. Its birthmarks. Our church has humanitarian missions. I traveled. To Yugoslavia. To the Caucasus. To Syria. I've seen concentration camps and could not open their gates. I've seen ravines full of corpses felled by bullets. Men killed by soldiers in a field, tossed naked into snow. A village after a chemical attack. People hid in the cellars, but the gas still got to them. The children there have olive skin. But when they got them out of the cellars, they were white. Waxen. The birthmarks of evil. I have seen them."

"Enough. I believe you." Kalitin wanted the priest to shut up. He could guess where that gas had come from. To stop Travniček's train of thought, to confuse him, he asked, "Tell me, what happened to your face? Did you get sick during the travels? They have horrible infections in the East."

"I was expecting your question," Travniček replied calmly. "Well, I'll tell you. It will help you understand me better."

CHAPTER 19

Shershnev had seen real concentration camps. Of course, in Chechnya they were called filtration points by the Russians, built hastily on the territory of some half-ruined factory, as long as there was a high fence. Sometimes it was just in a field: four towers and a row of barbed wire stretched between poles.

But he had never seen a museum on the site of a former camp. An old fortress, earthen ramparts, sturdy brick forts. Casemates that served as cells.

It was drizzling. They wandered around, not knowing where to go, pretending to be reading the information panels.

Things couldn't be stupider. Shershnev felt scammed. How had Grebenyuk put it? The adhesion was growing supernaturally. Or maybe the major hadn't said it, Shershnev had thought it himself? Why was he here? They were being led around the woods by a forest spirit. It was rational to admit it. Impossible to ignore the facts.

But then Shershnev was lost. In his experience there wasn't a single hint of a possible explanation.

All he could retrieve from his memory was the depressing astonishment with which he watched Charlie Chaplin movies as a child. Especially the one about the boxer. Shershnev had been in a boxing club, one run by the lightweight Sheredega, former army champion, winner of national prizes, and Shershnev was not one of his worst students. Sheredega later wrote a recommendation for admission to the special military school.

So when Shershnev watched the puny Chaplin mock his strong opponent, who should have destroyed him with the first punch, he helplessly made fists and regretted that he was not in the ring, for he would have shown him how it was done!

Shershnev could remember nothing more than this jester's magic of slipping away, where the clown wins because all the twists and ducks are on his side, because the art of comedy is based on a continuous violation of the everyday, the usual, the correct. It was a parallel, but not an explanation.

The policemen who had shown them the way actually accompanied them to the memorial parking lot. They waved. But instead of leaving, they sat at a cafe table under an umbrella and ordered something from the waitress. They could see the entire parking lot from their seats. There was no place to hide, anyway, nothing but empty fields all around. Grebenyuk took out a pack of cigarettes, and they lit up, hoping that the police would have a cup of coffee and move on. But the waitress returned with a tray: two huge hamburgers and fries; big portions. She set down the plates and joined them at the table, smoking; she said something and they laughed—they could hear it, even though the wind was blowing in the other direction.

"This is going to take a while," Grebenyuk said grimly.

The cops looked at them. The senior officer waved toward the gates—that's where to go.

"Let's go," Shershnev commanded in a doomed voice. "The sooner we start, the sooner we'll finish."

So they wandered within the fortress walls, occasionally encountering other visitors. They wanted to sit in one place, but noticed the video cameras—who knew? Maybe they would send someone to see what was wrong.

Good thing we have no direct contact with the bosses, Shershnev thought. What would they report? How could they explain the delay? A museum visit? If this nonsense were revealed, they'd be thrown out of the department. They'd be lucky to keep their jobs. But that would be later. They'd be able to talk themselves out of it. Make up some story about car trouble, anything at all, the main thing was to break out of here, get back on the trail.

Shershnev was also worried about Grebenyuk. His partner was quiet. Probably planning his report, the bastard. He had to get the major on his side, get him to agree to any story he made up.

Shershnev could ask for help from the embassy resident spies. He could get money, satellite data, weapons. He was used to being a particle of state power. Now that power was being wasted, seeping into sand, and it was pointless calling for help—help against what? Against Charlie Chaplin? Mr. Bean?

He was suffocating. They had agreed to spend a half hour at the museum. Long enough for the cops to leave. It had been nineteen minutes.

Grebenyuk came around a corner, calm, collected. He stopped two steps away and looked at the ceiling, the simple, gray showerheads, high up out of reach. Shershnev realized that he was in a former gas chamber. There was the heavy steel door on wheels. He wanted to leave, but Grebenyuk carefully held him back with his hand on his chest.

"Listen, Lieutenant Colonel."

Shershnev instinctively looked toward the door. Thank God, the cameras did not record sound. Basically, Grebenyuk was in his hands now. Breaking cover. If he reported that the major called him by rank in a public place, Grebenyuk would be arrested. Was he losing his mind?

But Grebenyuk looked perfectly fine, actually.

"Listen, Lieutenant Colonel," he repeatedly softly. "This seems a good place for a quiet talk."

Shershnev was taller, stronger. And he had had different training. He moved close and whispered an order.

"Shut it! Let's go!"

"Hang on," Grebenyuk said, raising his hands in a conciliatory manner. "We both feel that something's wrong. I'm a technical man. We have strict rules. If things aren't working, we have to find the reason."

"That's the point, you're a techie," Shershnev stressed the word. "But you're talking nonsense."

"Technology teaches you a lot of things," Grebenyuk said. "Has it ever happened to you that the car won't start, even though everything is fine? And then, it just starts? As if it had been waiting for something?"

Shershnev nodded reluctantly.

"That's what I'm talking about." Grebenyuk locked his fingers and then massaged them. "We like to say that if something that's supposed to work doesn't work, the reason is either at the entrance or the exit. I had this happen once. Came in to give advice. Two attempts, two failures. Detonators wouldn't work. They had checked everything of course, and not like the usual slapdash. Well, I was sent in to check for sabotage. It was very strange. I checked—couldn't have done it better myself. At the test site, it works. On location, it doesn't. I thought and said: send in another team. The technology is fine. Something's wrong with the man. They said: Is this official? I said: officially I will write that the technology is in order and the reason for failure is not clear. But you better send in new people. They did, and what do you think? It blew up perfectly. But the guy was still alive. His bodyguards covered him. He was alive. His bearded god was powerful."

Grebenyuk looked away and chuckled.

"Six months later a conscript shot him. Eighteen years old. Wet behind the ears, just out of training. Couldn't tell a rifle from his ass. The sergeants sent him into the woods for walnuts. The smarter privates buy them at the market and say they picked them. This brainless goof went into the woods. You know how these expeditions usually end."

Shershnev knew. He'd seen videos that soldiers passed around on cassettes. Later they appeared on the Internet. He didn't know that Grebenyuk had also been there, in the mountains, and now he felt a closeness to him, as if they had pledged friendship over drinks.

"So this guy should have been bumped off in front of a camera. Or sold into slavery. Who would pay the ransom for the conscript?" Grebenyuk stopped. "Instead, he killed three men with a single round. I don't know how it happened, he said. He didn't know who they were. He just shot because he was scared."

"So you think it's because of us?" Shershnev asked directly.

"Or him." Grebenyuk pointed beyond the mountains. "Or us and him. Tell me," Grebenyuk asked, "is there any special trail leading to you? You know what I mean?"

"There isn't, major," Shershnev responded firmly. "Let's get out of here. We'll take care of him."

They went past the blocks and casemates, past the execution wall to the gates. Children in colorful jackets were coming in, a school excursion. Some gathered around their teacher, others talked, giggled, took selfies in front of the cells.

Shershnev remembered what he had read quickly. Trains from the West and trains to the East. Starvation. Crematoriums. The remains of thousands of prisoners thrown into the river.

He felt the double irrationality of what was happening, the way you sometimes see a double halo around the sun.

What was done here had been committed by villains he had dreamed of fighting when he was a kid.

But now, looking at the renovated wooden towers, the faded black-and-white faces in the photos—he couldn't help remembering what he had seen himself: the same watchtowers, crowded cells stuffed with prisoners, the same black-and-white, filthy, overgrown faces.

Shershnev knew that they had been doing something else there. Unpleasant but necessary. There the people behind the barbed wire were enemies, not victims.

But still, the visual resemblance was so painfully obvious that it pushed Shershnev up against the wall.

The children posting on Instagram merely doubled the degree of absurdity. They behaved as if the past could never touch them:

not the distant past of this place, not Shershnev's recent past. He wanted desperately to show them that their insouciance was in vain; to stun them, overwhelm them with a random, painful confession. Smear them in real dirt. But suddenly the teacher finished her explanation and noticed the two men. She regarded them calmly, and Shershnev sensed she was like a mother hen; everyone in the field of her vague vision was a child. She was tied to them. She loved them and knew something about them, carefree and laughing indecently in a place of death, that Shershnev would never know. Knew and would protect them. Marina used to look like that.

The policemen were gone from the parking lot. Grebenyuk pulled out onto the road. The clouds were thinning, and a pale light glowed above the hills, revealing the way.

CHAPTER 20

This was their third hour together.

The pastor spoke, Kalitin half listened, uttering banalities as needed. Travniček was blathering about some theological nonsense. He never did answer the question about what happened to his face. But Kalitin no longer cared.

The desire to mock the pastor was long gone. The acute fear, the euphoria of possible salvation, were replaced by a dreary, enervating, conscious horror.

That horror used to appear sometimes in the early years of his defection. Kalitin could not fall asleep, worried that there was no place on earth to hide. He would get in the car, drive down twisting forest roads, imagining a pack of hounds on his tracks. The horror weakened with time and then vanished. Kalitin thought he had been cured, had deceived his curse. He couldn't understand why it had returned now, when he was so vulnerable. Where did that fateful precision come from?

"As a youth, I could not understand why God allows help for the unrighteous," Travniček was saying, and Kalitin listened, hoping to lose himself in the flow of words. It was getting dark. In five hours or so he could go back to the house. Kalitin hoped they had not shown up yet. But as soon as he imagined the path, they appeared: hiding behind bushes and trees, waiting beyond the turn in the road. Gray, faceless.

"My father was a Nazi," Travniček continued, and Kalitin nodded wearily. "Not a fellow traveler. A real Nazi. He was arrested after the war and quickly released. His friends helped. So he held on to his convictions until his death. When I told him I was going to be a priest, he replied: at least, you won't marry a Jewess. The dean of this church," Travniček gestured at the vaults, "also helped criminals."

Kalitin was waiting for Travniček to say something about the house on the hill. He was ready to say he knew nothing about it.

Travniček sighed.

"You asked about my face," he said, and Kalitin knew he was in for a piteous story of how God failed to heal his faithful servant yet also helps villains. The story was transparent and petty, and Kalitin felt a sense of relief.

"It's a long story," Travniček said. "I'll just tell you the end, otherwise even the whole night wouldn't be enough. As I told you, they watched me for a very long time." Kalitin felt shivers from the way the priest said "they." "It all began because I let young people meet at the church, to talk. That's when they started a case against me. They were in no hurry, they tried various methods. Essentially, over the years I got used to them. But then it all changed."

Travniček took a long pause. Kalitin found himself listening attentively.

"A parishioner started recording my sermons," he continued. "He didn't tell me about it. He let his friends make copies. They passed them on to others. Suddenly those cassettes multiplied, distributed on their own. Like an epidemic. Like a fire. Both believers and nonbelievers listened to them. At home. In church groups. In clubs. The police found them in searches, customs officers—in packages and luggage. The recordings were sent over the Wall. They were broadcast on Western radio. Day after day. It was very strange hearing my voice on the radio. I didn't understand. I was never a good orator. I just preached as usual. But apparently people heard something in them that I could not. The true Word of God."

Travniček stroked his lips with his fingers.

"I was frightened," he said softly and firmly. "Newspapers in the West began writing about me. Calling me a martyr. Even a 'true saint.'" Travniček spoke the last words in a half whisper. "Blasphemy!"

Kalitin found he understood the pastor. He had been called the "hope of science" at a party meeting, appointed to honorable presidiums. He just waited for them to end so that he could get back to his lab. The horror was easing, as if the eccentric pastor's story had chased away the killers' wandering shadows.

"They, of course, got really worried. Decided that I was making the recordings. They called me in for a chat. I tried to explain that I had nothing to do with it. Of course, they didn't believe me. Who would? It was essentially a miracle. A real miracle."

Weakling, Kalitin thought with pleasure. A little pressure, and he gave in. Kalitin liked the idea that his own fear was much more justified.

"They came to the church," Travniček said. "They wanted to find where I had the machinery. Which parishioners were helping.

They couldn't find a thing. Yet the recordings kept appearing. New ones. People were converting. Going to churches. Many people. Hundreds. Thousands."

Kalitin sensed that this story would have a double bottom, that it was leading where he didn't want to go—but the words had him in their power.

"They brought in experts," Travniček said. "Scientists. The town had an institute where they developed audio equipment. Eavesdropping devices among them. They studied the tapes. Their suggestion was to get some agents in civilian clothes inside the church during the sermon. The agents had special whistles, almost beyond human hearing, that the tape would record. Their orders were to blow the whistles every thirty seconds. They intended to get the cassette with the sermon. By comparing the times and volume of the whistles, which would also be recorded, they would be able to determine who had a tape recorder and where. Their photographer took pictures from the choir balcony. I saw the photographs later. In them, the church was divided up by marker lines like a chessboard. The agents were numbered. An invisible net."

Travniček looked around the church vault. Kalitin thought: that must be what the pastor meant when he spoke of creativity in the name of evil. Kalitin was amused once again: such big words for a banal case of acoustic surveillance, and not of the highest quality, incidentally! He automatically took the story as yet another puzzle and began thinking if there could be a chemical solution to the problem: radioactive markers, for example, or a marking spray. His normal thinking process reinvigorated him somewhat; he felt even more clearly that Travniček was playing a game with him.

"The scientists were sure they would succeed," said the pastor. "However, it turned out that the whistles were not recorded on the cassette. The sermon was easy to hear. 'The effect of church acoustics.' That was the conclusion of the report."

He must think that God had helped him, thought Kalitin. He liked his own skepticism; but he sensed that he was protecting himself, guarding against hearing faith through the words. For a moment he thought that the pastor and the killers were part of an absurd dream, a series of damned dreams that flowed into one another.

"So they changed tactics," Travniček continued sadly. "I was living in the parish house. One morning someone was at the door. I thought it would be them. But it was a messenger from the bakery. He had brought twenty cakes. I thought it was a joke. I had several friends quite capable of that. It was my address, my name, and the purchase was paid for. I gave the cakes to poor families. Happy that they would have a celebration. But then . . ."

Travniček stopped talking.

Kalitin waited.

"The next morning they delivered rakes. Ten packs. I grew suspicious. I wanted to send them back, but the deliveryman was gone." Travniček reached into his cassock and pulled out an old, worn notebook. "I always carry it with me. As a reminder."

He leafed through the pages, pointing:

"Dog cages. Fish food. Bicycles. Pumps. Three loads of coal. Sneakers. Hair dye. Mattresses. Axes. Suspenders. Shoe polish. Tape recorders. Televisions. Washing machines. Basins. Hats. Picture frames. Needles. Nails. Tables. Umbrellas. Potted seedlings. Couches. Gas lawn mowers. Milking equipment. Ship models in bottles. Hay. Pots and pans."

Kalitin felt the heavy weight of the listed objects.

Travniček continued. "No one would take the things back. The house turned into a warehouse. I couldn't give it all away—what if someone demanded it be returned? The rumor was that I had lost my mind. Become a hoarder. But I continued giving my sermons. They made a radiant path through the madness."

"Torture by abundance," Kalitin said. He had never heard of it, but he believed it unequivocally.

"Yes," Travniček said. "Then they started answering advertisements in my name. If something very large was for sale, for instance, a motorboat or grand piano. People would deliver the goods. Have arguments. One beat me up. I knew that they were doing it all. But it still seemed inexplicable, supernatural; who was I for them to expend so much effort, so much money?"

Kalitin imagined the fat, clumsy priest trying to explain things to the boat seller. It wasn't funny.

"Thank you for listening so kindly," Travniček said. "I think they had calculated very carefully. Anyone would break, think it was God's will. God's damnation. I wanted to run away. Drop everything and run."

Kalitin shuddered.

"But they knew that," Travniček said. "Next, they delivered chickens. Cages of chickens. They were left at the doorstep, and I couldn't leave them to die. There was chicken feed among earlier shipments. Then they sent tropical fish in tanks. Parrots. White lab mice."

Kalitin fell back into the past. White mice—so many had

died on the Island, dozens, hundreds of thousands, no one kept count, they incinerated the bodies and that was it.

Travniček's artless tale induced a strange stupor. His vision became multidimensional, he could see the killers' gray shadows in the distance, himself surrounded by church walls, and the past affairs of the Island.

"They kept dying anyway. I couldn't take care of them all," Travniček said bitterly. "Dying. I could find homes for the fish, chickens, and parrots. But hundreds of mice? So when they sent me dummies instead of animals, I was pleased. They didn't need to be fed."

"Dummies?" Kalitin echoed.

"Yes, dummies," Travniček confirmed. "Plastic. The kind in store windows. Naked. Female."

Kalitin thought of what he never thought about, what he had left back on the Island. Dummies.

If he could, he would have run out of the church. But the killers' shadows were waiting for him. And here the clever priest was mocking him. Dummies. Zakharyevsky once said: officially there aren't any here and never were. Aren't and never were, Kalitin repeated. Aren't and never were.

"They were stacked up," Travniček continued. "Pink. It had started snowing in the morning. They had eyes. Plastic blue eyes with lashes."

Kalitin did not remember the eyes. The bodies had not been pink. White, gray, blue. Color sometimes returned afterward. On the morgue table.

"I should have guessed that it was a warning. I just brought them inside. Ten naked, plastic women in a priest's house. I was afraid I would be photographed with them, that they had rented the apartment across the way. That would have been a fine photo."

Women. They were not given women. Kalitin had asked: gender differences in the organism, he explained, different biochemistry. He needed to test. But the ones at the top did not want to hear it. Their half-hearted determination drove Kalitin crazy.

"Then it all stopped. That was even worse. Torture by absence. I had gotten used to the madness, began to find some strength in it. I lasted eleven days. On the twelfth I asked for death if God did not want to protect me. I broke. I stopped preaching. For the arrows of the Almighty are within me, the poison whereof drinketh up my spirit: the terrors of God do set themselves in array against me," he chanted. "Job 6:4."

Kalitin looked at the priest. He derived fierce pleasure from seeing his face.

"Here's what I looked like then." Travniček handed him a photo from the leather pocket in the notebook.

Kalitin was stunned. He could not have imagined the elegant and spiritual appearance of the former Travniček; thin, aristocratic, with a high forehead. Gentle, aloof, and at the same time willful. Handsome. Very handsome. Focused on a high, unearthly goal.

Women must have fallen for him in droves, Kalitin thought, trying to demean the image he had seen.

"I started drinking then," Travniček said. "At home, naturally. There was always an open bottle in the cupboard. The source of the Word had dried up, and I sought another. I knew what was happening. The recordings, the cassettes, vanished; people stopped listening to them, as if the wind had died down. The storm was over. So I drank more. 'Their wine is the poison of dragons, and the cruel venom of asps.'" He spoke majestically.

Kalitin looked up again. Looked at the scaly mask. Now he could see the face behind it.

"Their wine is the poison of dragons," Travniček said thoughtfully. "I took only one sip from the glass. The usual taste, the usual pinot gris, Grauburgunder. You know the one I mean. Then there was pain. In my whole body at once. It's not surprising that the people who consider others saboteurs, who care about the purity of the race, come up with the idea of modifying pesticides." Travniček named the substance.

Kalitin saw black. He knew it. Not Neophyte, but still an ultimate poison. The man was a living corpse. Nothing could save you from that substance, not pumping the stomach, not blood transfusions. There were no antidotes. Kalitin knew that as firmly as two times two equals four.

His mind, his solid rational world cracked. Through it was the unknown.

Apparently unaware of what was happening to Kalitin, he went on. "They told me I was an anomalous occurrence. I was supposed to die. And in fact, I did. My former self was dead. I gave sermons later. Ordinary words. No miracle in them. As for my face, the doctors said it was a hormonal reaction. That may be so. Physically. But it is a mark. God's mark."

Kalitin reeled.

Travniček's face floated before his eyes. It changed rapidly: human, animal, stone, forest, snake, a multilayered, composite mask. All the dead creatures poisoned by Kalitin were resurrected in it. Horses. Goats. Dogs. Monkeys. Rats. Mice. People.

The last face to rise out of the vortex, from the depths, to flash and fade, was Vera's.

Kalitin imagined that the resurrected souls sought to settle in him: there was no refuge for them except the body of their murderer. He felt his own face turn to stone, while Travniček's became human again.

The pastor embraced him. Patted his head.

Kalitin could tell that the pastor was not lying. Travniček was the miracle that crossed out Kalitin's destiny, rendered Neophyte meaningless, insignificant. It had aimed for absolute power over matter, and the absolute was destroyed. Kalitin tried to persuade himself that Neophyte would have killed the priest and saw that the irrationality of a miracle was higher than his thinking, plans, calculations.

He was conquered; he was filled with deathly hatred. Kalitin wanted to kill the priest; he had only one weapon at hand. Kalitin began whispering, telling the pastor the blackest and most evil things that had happened to him—his own life; pouring it into Travniček like poison. Kalitin could not pause, unstoppering all the secrets of the past as if they had been sealed in test tubes and ampoules, shouting without hearing what he was shouting, so that the wonderful pastor would swallow the poisonous revelation and die like the mice and dogs, apes and humans, Kazarnovsky and Vera—the death of creatures. Death without miracles.

CHAPTER 21

Only now, on the mountain road, did Shershnev appreciate that Grebenyuk was a real master. Minute by minute, the major was stubbornly regaining the time stolen by the police.

Cliff-face on the left. On the right, warning stripes, then an abyss. The flat yellow lamps in the tunnel—the car flew without resistance, the wipers flipping once in a while to remove bugs from the windshield, the headlight cutting through the dusk, and the golden disco music of his adolescence played softly, a melody from the eighties, "Modern Talking."

Shershnev had never felt so acutely the exchange of space for time, an exchange in their favor, as if Grebenyuk were paying generously from the pocket of his future successes.

The white arrows in the lanes said forward! Forward! The road rose higher toward the pass, the former border.

The tunnel. Narrowed to two lanes. Grebenyuk did not slow down, turn, turn. The bright red scattering of stop signals up ahead. The car stopped. They could hear the exhaust fans on the concrete ceilings. They were trapped inside the mountain.

Other cars drove in behind them and the drivers obediently

turned off their engines. Grebenyuk tried the radio: nothing but static on every station.

They looked at each other—both faces betraying concern. Shershnev got out and knocked on the window of the car in front. Three guys, students probably, were smoking—and not tobacco. He could smell weed.

"Do you know what happened?" he asked. "Is there a long wait?"

The driver laughed and said in a blurry, happy voice, "It's the mountains, man. Something's always happening here. Want a hit?" he offered the joint.

He went down the row of cars. No one knew anything. Mobile phones didn't work, GPS systems turned themselves off. Shershnev noticed a phone on the wall, a red box with the emergency sign. He picked up the receiver and pushed the button: *beep, beep.* Long beeps. No answer.

People sat in their cars, calm, obedient. Sheep, thought Shershnev. He remembered how their convoy once ran into a herd of thousands of sheep in a ravine. The shepherd gloated as he looked at the military vehicles trapped in the river of sheep, which headed down, paying no attention to the blaring horns, leaving bits of wool on the trucks. Stupid, obedient creatures. Like these people. They wouldn't let him through, wouldn't move aside. They would just wait.

He went back.

"Too bad we didn't bring the siren light," Grebenyuk said. The joke died like a bad match. The cooling hood creaked. They lacked the strength to think, compare, build suppositions.

Shershnev had no problem in enclosed spaces. Reverse

claustrophobia, their doctor called it. He went down into tight forest caches, underground irrigation canals turned into secret pathways, he wandered for days through the damp tunnels of a former missile base that the enemy had turned into a lair. Stone did not scare him, tightness and dark did not scare him, nor did stale air low on oxygen.

But here, in the dry, well-lit tunnel with evacuation hatches, he felt uncomfortable underground for the first time. The smell of gasoline and exhaust pushed into his nose, and the cliff seemed to push down on him from above, like a press.

Duplicitous stone, its unreliable solidity! So many times he had seen huge boulders fallen on the road, smoldering cars buried beneath them, round spots of soot from wheels, burned and tossed aside by the explosion, human heads . . . or that tunnel in 2008. The mountains there were much higher. Narrow tunnel without light, filled with diesel exhaust, the dull headlights of tanks, and it felt like the ceiling would collapse from the roar of the engines, the fear of the armored bodies the drivers were urging into the narrow funnel, too narrow for two vehicles, in the mountain.

The air was so wonderful on the other side—neither the fires nor the smell of death spoiled its purity, divine purity! They got through, they did, Shershnev told himself.

Red lights flashed ahead. The head of the bottleneck slowly began to move.

It was dark outside. The cars stopped again. Shershnev got out, swallowed the icy, raw air, redolent of mountain wildness. Along the distant spurs, red stars blinked on electric wind turbines, and clumps of thick fog crawled along the road. The headlights dissolved in the vapor, creating an unnatural, otherworldly reflection.

Shershnev shook his head. Had he breathed in some weed?

The cars moved. Beyond the turn lay the former border between Czech territory and Germany. Abandoned control posts. Empty duty-free stores. A police helicopter blocked the road. Traffic officers directed the cars to the former border parking lot.

This is for us, Shershnev first thought.

But he quickly changed his mind: they would have done this differently. They would have stopped only their car, brought in the special forces. These were ordinary policemen, not even equipped with bulletproof vests.

Grebenyuk pulled up by a policeman and opened the window.

"Avalanche," the overwhelmed traffic cop shouted. "It's the rain. They'll open the road by morning. They're working on it now. Wait in the parking lot. If you need fuel, there's a gas station twenty kilometers below, you'll have time." He waved his lit baton.

The truck drivers settled down in their cabs. Car drivers folded down their rear seats. Grebenyuk parked at the very exit of the lot. Right, thought Shershnev. The whole herd will head for the exit in the morning, and we have to be first.

He suddenly realized how tired and hungry he was.

"Let's go look around," he said.

"Wouldn't hurt to get some food," Grebenyuk replied. "We've worked up an appetite."

They walked past empty kiosks with faded posters inside. Plump dark-red lips and golden lipstick. Tropical palms, a beauty in a bikini, a bottle of whisky on a bar. Pearl earrings on black velvet. A light blue bottle, resembling a sail, of men's cologne, discontinued long ago.

Shershnev looked over at Grebenyuk, who gently touched his inside pocket: the container is here, I took it as per orders, don't worry.

Empty flagpoles jangling in the wind. The hum of a transformer hut. And there was a hot dog stand, dusty metal blinds, rain-blurred menu in a currency that no longer existed. A grocery store. A pile of ice-cream freezers. An umbrella with protruding ribs. A dog ran out of the dark, a skinny, mangy mutt, with a beseeching look; it wagged its stumpy tail, inviting them to follow. A light flickered in the far end of the lot.

None of the drivers headed in that direction, as if they knew there was a very good reason not to do so. Or they were just used to flying past at high speed and had no memories of the area.

There was a huge sign for a hotel; once the sign had burned with hundreds of bulbs, now there was only one left in a bottom corner. They shrugged and headed into the darkness. There was a weak smell of habitation, food.

Beyond the trees and the living hedge once trimmed and now wild, stood a building. A hotel at the border—so many benches in the garden, enough for a hundred people. The place was dying now, the benches covered in leaves. But there was still light in the first-floor windows.

Shershnev opened the door.

The slot machine rang and shook, red hearts and green apples jumping. A fat barmaid smoked at the bar, the smoke rising to the ceiling, stained as yellow as wax paper. Her pendulous breasts were enormous, as if she breastfed the children of mountain giants. Drinking beer across from her was an old rocker with straggly gray hair, thin, dried out, wrapped in black leather; his legs and arms were unnaturally straight, as if he were a puppet and the maker had forgotten the joints. Someone in the corner was hidden by a newspaper, only the top of his head visible.

An old, fuzzy television set played above the counter. Little figures ran wanly in a field; even from a distance you could see that they were second-rate teams, a second division, the last chance, bowlegged failures who no longer expected anything from the game or themselves.

Shershnev grimaced fastidiously and turned to leave. But he sensed that the place suited the day; here, in the forgotten hotel, nothing more could happen to them. Everything here had happened once and for all twenty years ago.

The waitress came out from the counter. She had thin legs that didn't seem strong enough to hold her heavy body. She doesn't know about the landslide, the closed road, the overfilled parking lot, the hundreds of people nearby who could bring her a year's salary, thought Shershnev.

"Two beers," Grebenyuk said.

She went behind the bar. The tap handle shuddered in death throes. Thick, sticky foam came out of the spout, splashing the glasses and the counter. She turned the handle hastily, but the tap hissed and spat and then shut up with a thin moan.

A newspaper fell down, revealing a full-page crossword all filled in. The man, apparently the son of the barmaid and the old man, a strange hybrid of bloods living near the border, big belly and rickety arms and legs, walked past them slowly, opened the hatch, stuffed his body into the cellar, made some noise there, and pushed out a cold barrel.

"Freak show," Grebenyuk said quietly. "Should we risk eating here?"

Shershnev looked at the menu and chose safe-looking sausages and fried potatoes.

She brought the beer. Shershnev pointed at the picture of the sausages, but she shook her head and pointed at what they had. Steak.

Shershnev nodded.

The beer was icy cold, moderately bitter, amazingly fresh, as if they had a mountain beer spring under the floor. They gulped down half a mug each, lit up.

Beer on an empty stomach softened his thinking, and everything seemed blurry and habitual: the long ribbons of flypaper with flies from years ago, the dilatory game between two losing teams, the gurgling trills of the slot machine. The subject was very close, on the other side of the mountains, and Shershnev stopped thinking about him; let him sleep. The meeting would come soon enough.

The waitress went through the faded, hole-ridden curtain, and started banging pans. The old man gave them a questioning look, bent over the bar, and poured two more glasses.

"I remember similar weirdness," Grebenyuk said, taking a sip. "It was in an old kebab place. The kind from our childhood. We were eating shashlik. We had thrown a sheep into our trunk along the road. Even the bar with its glasses and trays was intact. With aluminum forks that bend when you try to pierce the meat."

Shershnev had a sip. He had eaten with forks like that in the garrison dining hall, when his father took him there.

"The most important thing was not to look out the window. We were in the city after the second storming. Ruins. For some reason only the little place survived. Even the sign was intact."

Shershnev nodded. He also remembered that town, sooty, scorched, shelled—but with the same signs, stores, lampposts, bus stops, buses, like home. That was the strangest thing: trying to find the familiar in the ruins. He remembered that cafe, too— they had passed it several times. So that means, their paths had crossed, he thought. They had a connection.

They clinked glasses.

His stomach rumbled. Shershnev looked around, found the right door. In the hallway a machine dispensing cigarettes and condoms, long-empty, hung on the wall. There was a chlorinated toilet smell, the smell of solitude. At the military school the only place you could be alone was on the john. And only after classes. He lowered his trousers, sat, and happily emptied the contents of his churning gut. Even the tank was ancient, attached to the wall with a porcelain handle on a chain.

Shershnev pulled on it. No water.

"My shit," he said, looking into the toilet. He realized he was drunk, intoxicated by a glass and a half, like a kid. He slammed down the lid and went back—let the owners deal with it. He rinsed his hands and wiped them on his trousers. There were no towels here.

Grebenyuk had started eating. Rare steak. First-class veal. Shershnev knew about meat. The major had eaten half of a large chop, bloody juice dripping from the corner of his mouth. Shershnev cut off a piece from the edge and started chewing—fresh meat, where do they get it here? He cut off another piece, put it in his mouth, and he imagined the meat was mooing, mooing terribly and sadly. Shershnev dropped the fork, and Grebenyuk said, laughing, "I almost choked. There's a damned cowshed on the other side of the wall. They keep animals."

Shershnev looked at the blood seeping out of the meat. At the tiny rosemary needles. He was dizzy.

"You don't like it rare?" Grebenyuk asked genially. "Not everyone does. I do. Ask the woman, she'll cook it some more. Though that's bad for the meat, it will be tough."

"Yes, I prefer it well-done," Shershnev interrupted. "Let's have another beer."

They clinked glasses again.

When the bill came, Shershnev realized he had forgotten the pin code for Ivanov's credit card.

He remembered everything: old email passwords, code words to communicate with the embassy, phone numbers, but those four digits kept slipping away, showing off when he tried to visualize them, the six turned into an eight, the seven into a two, the three into an eight and back again.

The old woman had brought in an old payment processing device and waited silently. Grebenyuk got out his card and smoothly entered his code; Shershnev realized how hard the day had been on him, if he had forgotten the number that he himself had chosen and connected to some date or event.

The old woman led them upstairs, unlocked a room that was unexpectedly clean and cozy. Two beds by the walls, standing lamps, a wardrobe, an embroidered tapestry on the wall: hunters trumpeting, a dying stag at their feet.

Shershnev undressed and set his watch alarm for six. He fell asleep hearing Grebenyuk turning in his bed, the squeaking of old springs compacted by hundreds of bodies.

He knew tomorrow all would be well.

CHAPTER 22

Neophyte.

Kalitin left for his house to get the substance; the pastor could not stop him. The word remained in the church's dusky interior.

So familiar. So far away.

Neophyte.

It reminded Travniček of his early years in the ministry. The first confessions he had heard. There were so many later on, brief and lengthy, eloquent and forced, sincere—and false from first word to the last . . . In forest villages, in mining settlements, in workers' cities, he essentially read books of other people's sins, saw the same birthmarks of evil, its monotonous faces. He learned to see the simple rules, unsophisticated themes, the particular features as clear as the signs of a profession, work calluses that differed in miners and loggers, carpenters and fishermen. He figured out the logic of the calendar: sins of autumn and spring, winter and summer; sins of poverty and wealth; vice and injured virtue, past and future; sins of strength and weakness, power and slavery, hope and despair, love and loathing.

There were few confessions he could remember; probably for the best, thought Travniček. His memory was sound, and pastoral service had never become a routine; but once he released people from their sins, he did not keep them inside himself. They vanished, leaving behind empty, identical husks of words.

There was only one confession he knew almost by heart; it sounded inside him unspoken.

Franz. An old man, a former soldier. He had a beer hall and was chairman of a hunting club; every autumn, hunters gathered at his bar and drove to the distant bulrush lakes—and then returned to lay out rows of geese and ducks in the backyard. The next day Franz would come to church; he smelled of beer and singed feathers. Travniček was young then, and Franz always tried to take a dig at him, blame him for his inexperience. The former priest, Father Haschke, had understood him better and performed the service with befitting dignity. His sins were simple and strictly doled out, like an old man's shots of schnapps.

Before death, Franz called for him. The old man lived in one section of the beer hall, in the back rooms. When Travniček arrived, the bar was full of the noisy regulars, billiard balls cracking and cash register ringing; the pastor was offended by this marked contempt for the mystery of death. Franz lay in a bed, unexpectedly large for his desiccated body.

"The beach. It was at the beach," the old man said, and Travniček, truly still a student, a neophyte then, expected to hear a story about a long-ago salacious adventure by the sea, a seduced woman or girl.

"It was at the beach," Franz repeated. "They kept coming at me. What else could I do? Lieutenant Huber ordered us to open fire. So I shot. The bearer fed me the ammunition belt, and I shot."

Franz talked about the overheated barrel that had to be cooled; the thickness of the fortification concrete of their bunker; of how communications were interrupted; he told him about the long, long day. Travniček heard and saw only hundreds of American soldiers, jumping out of landing barges, running along the sand, and dying, dying, dying; he pictured the awful and empty tautology of evil, lasting and not lasting, reduced to a single movement of the machine gun's trigger.

"Our bunker was called 'Franz,'" the old man said. "I thought it was a good omen."

The old gunner died.

Now waiting for Kalitin to come back, Travniček thought about that story. He felt only exhaustion, immeasurable exhaustion. Kalitin's confession, the story of his life, had astonished the pastor—but not at all the way the chemist had wanted.

Travniček saw the same tautology, the chain reaction of evil; a pile of rotting fruit, infected by a black worm. He remembered all the things that had been sent to him—good things people needed, separated by an evil will from their purpose, turned—contrary to their essence—into weapons of torture; piled into a mountain of the meaningless.

Travniček knew that Kalitin would return. With his gas.

Well. He would wait here, in the church.

Neophyte.

How strange . . . Too bad Kalitin didn't know.

Neophyte.

That's what they called him in the operative file they had on him. Neophyte. The nickname the people from the gray house had given him. Others had more impressive, more colorful names:

Inspirer, Missionary, Fanatic, Captain, Pilgrim, Apostle, Prelate, Treasurer, Miser. That was revealed once the archives were opened.

When they started the file on him, they considered him a neophyte. A green boy. A beginner. Useless. The informers, the agents—he was Neophyte for them. A proper noun. That's what they wrote in every report, in every surveillance account, as if they were trying to make the nickname stick.

He hadn't wanted to request his file at first. He sensed how painful and bitter it would be. He was far from the thoughts of the pastors who had gone into politics; vengeance did not seem to be the direct work of human hands. But then he remembered the most obvious: "There is nothing hidden that will not be made known." He went to the archives; he wanted to know, for it was wrong to reject the truth. It didn't matter if there was not only truth but also lies and deceit in the papers of the gray house; only the side that was visible and beneficial to the spies. So what. He would know for whom to pray.

He saw his life through their eyes. An undemanding series of the commonplace. Because of the dry manner of narration, the days plucked out and added to the file were particularly similar to one another. But he could feel that even through the distilled monotony of reports, his torment, his insubordination, his work of resistance broke through in a way he had not seen before. He realized there in the archives how long he had not given up. It was a human miracle, and he had manifested it. He had renounced, but before that he had stood in the fire. There was no pride in that understanding and no justification.

Travniček did not look at his watch. Time decided nothing. He just had to be ready.

Long ago he had heard on the radio that Father Jerzy Popiełuszko had been recognized as a martyr. The pastor thought then of him and the many others killed—weren't they worthy of living until freedom? Until the prison was destroyed. They were his invisible interlocutors, the distant confessors of his thoughts. Why was the miracle of salvation manifested in him? He, who was worse. Unworthy.

"Others suffered mockery and beatings and shackles and prison. They were stoned, sawed, tortured, died by the sword," he told himself then. "And all of them commended in their faith did not receive what was promised. Because God foresaw in us something better, for without us they could not achieve perfection." It was then that he understood there was no point in looking for the devil's hand in their death, to talk about God's permission; there are times and countries that are like minefields, and the walker knows where he steps.

And now it was in them, in their unforeseen sacrifice that he saw his lighthouse, his support.

He fiercely regretted telling Kalitin he should make a public confession. He had overtaken the voice of conscience. He had been rash. He had been severe and insistent, tried too hard to persuade him. Then he realized that his regret was in vain; he did not know, could not know, what image would still appear to awaken conscience; how things would be resolved there, in the solitude of the night, between the fugitive and the Creator.

He could only wait.

CHAPTER 23

Kalitin stopped the car at the very beginning of the drive shaded by apple trees leading to the house. There were blackberry thickets here, which occasionally provided privacy for the parked cars of teenage couples.

These were his mountains once again. No shadows. He knew that Travniček had not lied, the agents had come, and killers could be lurking nearby. But he was no longer afraid of them, did not see the night as filled with immaterial ghosts.

The only one he feared was the pastor.

Kalitin sensed that he had not hurt, not even insulted the priest. He put his entire life into a single blow, a single confession—and it merely dissipated as if he had not existed. Nothing happened. The strength, the inner strength, everything that had accumulated, hardened, pressed, burned, driven—it vanished forever. Now there was only momentum. Idling in a meaningless direction.

An old counting rhyme came to mind, something they had all whispered excitedly at Uncle Igor's place before playing hide-and-seek.

Diddle diddle, one two three

You can't get away from me!
A bear runs here, a bear runs there,
There are bears everywhere!
Diddle diddle, three two one
Bears are out to have some fun.
One bear growls, one bear grins
One bear hides—guess who wins!

Even Vera's death did not horrify or repulse the pastor. His response burned Kalitin.

"Have you heard of Clara Immerwahr?" Travniček asked, as if he had the name ready at hand.

"No," Kalitin responded indifferently.

"Fritz Haber?" Travniček asked calmly.

"Yes," Kalitin replied carefully.

He knew the name from a special handbook with a tight thread sewn along the spine, so no pages could be removed unnoticed. When they were done studying it, they returned it to the safe in the special library. Haber. The father of nitrogen fertilizer—and the father of gas warfare, the grandfather of Zyklon B, invented in his laboratory.

"Clara was his wife. And also a chemist," Travniček said. "She tried to talk him out of it. When she learned that he was going to the front to oversee a gas attack, she shot herself in the heart. With his gun. No church approves of suicide. But I am not a good priest. There are times when one must not abet."

Travniček paused and then continued. "I think about the scientist who invented the poison used on me. About what you told me. It's not just ethics: thou shalt not kill. You think that by violating the ban on testing on humans you are advancing along the path to comprehension. Taking a short cut. But that's the point: the means begin to determine the goal. What you produce becomes a creation devoid of grace. The dimension of goodness. It is an act of the devil, I would say."

"One bear growls, one bear grins," whispered Kalitin. "One bear hides—guess who wins!"

He started the engine. He drove up to the house without fear. There was no one behind the trees in the dark, he felt sure of that. Maybe an hour earlier, an hour later, but not now.

The moon laid a path on the dewy grass.

Kalitin went down to the cellar, opened the safe, took out the steel box in which Neophyte slept. He opened it, for the first time in many years. A light blue bottle, looking like a wind-filled sail.

Kalitin carefully shut the box and placed it in a special attaché case that had a compartment with clasps, clicked the locks, thumbed the code wheels.

Slowly he picked up the case by the handle and set it on its bottom, feeling Neophyte flowing in the bottle, turning over in its sleep.

He unscrewed the body of his computer and took out the hard drive. That was it.

Kalitin put the attaché case on the backseat, fastening it with the safety belt.

The house. He looked back. The ceiling lamp was on in the study. Let it be. The ones who come will think he's there.

Kalitin remembered that he had left the light on in his hotel room when he went out into the night, to flee. The light was similar, yellow with an orange tinge. Long ago, forgotten. The lamp on father's desk had the same glow. He realized it was just a coincidence of visible spectrums but he had never felt such power, the inner meaning in a natural similarity of tones and shades.

An unbearable desire engulfed him: to break this chain of dead-end escapes. To go back to where he was still the boy stopped at the door of the Third Entrance.

The pine tree air freshener swayed in the windshield: diddle diddle, one two three.

He thought he didn't know where to go; he had forgotten the necessary turns, signs, the layout of the whole area. But he hit the gas; he couldn't sit inert, couldn't wait, couldn't believe in the possibility of salvation.

One bear hides—guess who wins!

Second gear. The road was uneven. No problem, he would drive slowly. It wasn't far to the asphalt.

Kalitin pictured Travniček, dead, clumsy in his cassock, collapsed in front of the altar, and opened the window to breath the bitter night air. He would get out of here. Go to a distant country. But first he had to get rid of the witness.

He thought he could smell success, the mindless, crafty success of fleeing fugitives who had followed these paths.

The front wheel hit a stone. The car bounced, the undercarriage cracked.

Kalitin fell asleep not knowing that he had died, as had the swallows, wood beetles, worms, woodlice, and moles. The car had rolled down the slope into a ditch, and the engine ceased in the moonlight. Neophyte vanished through the tiniest crack in the bottle's spray pump, flew off into the astral plane, lost among the atoms and molecules.

When the police car arrived, summoned by vigilant villagers who had seen the headlights shining motionlessly into the field, even the faintest odor had disappeared.

The police officer called at Travniček`s door; some of the villagers had reported seeing the solitary newcomer the previous day. With the priest.

It was still dark, with no trace of dawn.

Travniček was absolutely exhausted. He was waiting for the visitor to return.

But when he understood what happened, he thought about the men pursuing Kalitin. Men with hearts of steel. He was strangely sure they hadn't arrived yet. But the police didn't even know they were en route. It was up to Travniček to seal their fate.

He hesitated a bit. Recalled Kalitin's fear of the shadows chasing him. And merely said to the officer: It seems the story is not yet over . . .

Shershnev awoke before the alarm. Grebenyuk, hunched over, was vomiting in the toilet. His face was white.

"Shitty meat," the major rasped. "Unused to it. You were lucky. My insides are heaving. I can't drive."

Shershnev dressed. He put the container in his inside pocket.

"Wait here," he said. "I'll pick you up on the way back."

Grebenyuk threw up.

"Just don't call for an ambulance," Shershnev said. This situation didn't seem odd to him. He thought it was as it should be. It would be easier alone. The thought that Grebenyuk poisoned himself or was good at faking it flew by and vanished. No, the major was just unlucky. Something bad was bound to happen, and it did.

People were still sleeping at the parking lot. The helicopter was gone. Bulldozers crawled around the avalanche, moving boulders. One lane, marked with flags, was already open. A worker waved him on, and Shershnev hit the gas, enjoying the car's response.

He went down the serpentine pass and turned onto a side road. The valleys were still swirling with fog, even though the sun was rising over the ridges. It was the hour when animals awakened before the peasants, and Shershnev felt a new surplus of time, driving faster than Grebenyuk had the day before.

Here was the town. The first trolley was at the terminal. The driver was smoking and drinking coffee from a thermos. Yesterday's trees. Yesterday's houses. Yesterday's garbage in the can, even the traffic light was yesterday's; no one had seen it yet today, no one was awake, only Shershnev and that driver. The ticket validating device in the trolley was buzzing, setting today's date, but no one had yet had a fare card marked with the new stamp.

Turn to the right. Church on the hill. He would make it, as if yesterday's long day still continued.

A black figure. Must be the priest departing after a service. Who knows what their religion is, what time they start.

A priest on the road. Bad omen.

A turn, the apple tree alley, a fresh break in the bushes—a truck must have backed into it. A narrow valley. Everything was just as the agents had described. The subject must be asleep. Everyone was sleeping.

But one would not wake up.

When the helicopter rose over the forest and metallic voices addressed him, he had time to look back—an armored German police van was blocking the road.

He turned the car across the ditch up onto the hill. A light feeling of success carried him over stones and hummocks. The car struck the embankment and the motor stopped.

He ran toward the trees. The helicopter clattered overhead, the metal voices ordered him to stop. A round of bullets punctured the grass, but he managed to get into the woods. Dogs barked, he heard orders, shots. The forest spun him around, put roots and holes under his feet, lashed him with branches.

There was a sandy niche, a lair, under an overhang, and he crawled in, crazed by the running.

A gas grenade fell from above, hissing, scattering white, acid smoke. He could still activate the container, let Neophyte out; he tried to find it, at least touch it, feel that he had a weapon.

His pocket was empty. The bottle had fallen out along the way.

Weeping from the tear gas, he crawled out, covered in leaves like a forest demon.

A semicircle of soldiers in black gas masks aimed their weapons at him.

Shershnev slowly raised his hands.

More and more SWAT team soldiers ran out of the woods.

The barrels looked him in the face. The only visible face among dozens of black masks.

That evening it would be in all the papers. On television. On the Internet.

On the smartphone of the boy from the container.

On Maxim's smartphone.

Shershnev felt tears running down his cheeks, not tears of relief, but tears caused by the acrid gas.

SERGEI LEBEDEV has been called the most important younger Russian author writing today. His novels have been translated into many languages and three of his works—*Oblivion, The Year of the Comet* and *The Goose Fritz*—have been published in English to great acclaim by New Vessel Press.

ANTONINA W. BOUIS has translated over 80 works by Russian authors such as Evgeny Yevtushenko, Mikhail Bulgakov and Andrei Sakharov. Bouis, previously executive director of the Soros Foundation in the former USSR, now lives in New York City.

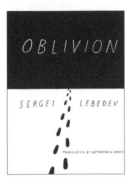

OBLIVION
BY SERGEI LEBEDEV

In one of the first 21st century Russian novels to probe the legacy of the Soviet prison camp system, a young man travels to the vast wastelands of the Far North to uncover the truth about a shadowy neighbor who saved his life, and whom he knows only as Grandfather II. Emerging from today's Russia, where the ills of the past are being forcefully erased from public memory, this masterful novel represents an epic literary attempt to rescue history from the brink of oblivion.

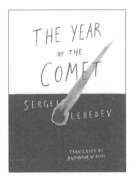

THE YEAR OF THE COMET
BY SERGEI LEBEDEV

A story of a Russian boyhood and coming of age as the Soviet Union is on the brink of collapse. Lebedev depicts a vast empire coming apart at the seams, transforming a very public moment into something tender and personal, and writes with stunning beauty and shattering insight about childhood and the growing consciousness of a boy in the world.

GOOSE FRITZ
BY SERGEI LEBEDEV

This revelatory novel tells the story of a young Russian, the sole survivor of a once numerous clan of German origin, who delves relentlessly into the unresolved past. *The Goose Fritz* illuminates both personal and political history in a passion-filled family saga about an often confounding country that has long fascinated the world.

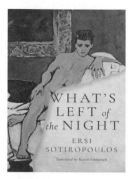

WHAT'S LEFT OF THE NIGHT
BY ERSI SOTIROPOULOS

Constantine Cavafy arrives in Paris in 1897 on a trip that will deeply shape his future and push him toward his poetic inclination. With this lyrical novel, tinged with an hallucinatory eroticism that unfolds over three unforgettable days, celebrated Greek author Ersi Sotiropoulos depicts Cavafy in the midst of a journey of self-discovery across a continent on the brink of massive change. A stunning portrait of a budding author—before he became C.P. Cavafy, one of the 20th century's greatest poets—that illuminates the complex relationship of art, life, and the erotic desires that trigger creativity.

THE 6:41 TO PARIS
BY JEAN-PHILIPPE BLONDEL

Cécile, a stylish 47-year-old, has spent the weekend visiting her parents outside Paris. By Monday morning, she's exhausted. These trips back home are stressful and she settles into a train compartment with an empty seat beside her. But it's soon occupied by a man she recognizes as Philippe Leduc, with whom she had a passionate affair that ended in her brutal humiliation 30 years ago. In the fraught hour and a half that ensues, Cécile and Philippe hurtle towards the French capital in a psychological thriller about the pain and promise of past romance.

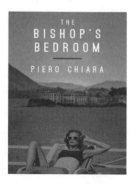

THE BISHOP'S BEDROOM
BY PIERO CHIARA

World War Two has just come to an end and there's a yearning for renewal. A man in his thirties is sailing on Lake Maggiore in northern Italy, hoping to put off the inevitable return to work. Dropping anchor in a small, fashionable port, he meets the enigmatic owner of a nearby villa. The two form an uneasy bond, recognizing in each other a shared taste for idling and erotic adventure. A sultry, stylish psychological thriller executed with supreme literary finesse.

THE EYE
BY PHILIPPE COSTAMAGNA

It's a rare and secret profession, comprising a few dozen people around the world equipped with a mysterious mixture of knowledge and innate sensibility. Summoned to Swiss bank vaults, Fifth Avenue apartments, and Tokyo storerooms, they are entrusted by collectors, dealers, and museums to decide if a coveted picture is real or fake and to determine if it was painted by Leonardo da Vinci or Raphael. *The Eye* lifts the veil on the rarified world of connoisseurs devoted to the authentication and discovery of Old Master artworks.

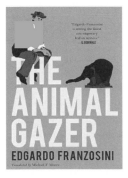

THE ANIMAL GAZER
BY EDGARDO FRANZOSINI

A hypnotic novel inspired by the strange and fascinating life of sculptor Rembrandt Bugatti, brother of the fabled automaker. Bugatti obsessively observes and sculpts the baboons, giraffes, and panthers in European zoos, finding empathy with their plight and identifying with their life in captivity. Rembrandt Bugatti's work, now being rediscovered, is displayed in major art museums around the world and routinely fetches large sums at auction. Edgardo Franzosini recreates the young artist's life with intense lyricism, passion, and sensitivity.

ALLMEN AND THE DRAGONFLIES
BY MARTIN SUTER

Johann Friedrich von Allmen has exhausted his family fortune by living in Old World grandeur despite present-day financial constraints. Forced to downscale, Allmen inhabits the garden house of his former Zurich estate, attended by his Guatemalan butler, Carlos. This is the first of a series of humorous, fast-paced detective novels devoted to a memorable gentleman thief. A thrilling art heist escapade infused with European high culture and luxury that doesn't shy away from the darker side of human nature.

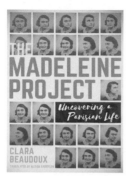

THE MADELEINE PROJECT
BY CLARA BEAUDOUX

A young woman moves into a Paris apartment and discovers a storage room filled with the belongings of the previous owner, a certain Madeleine who died in her late nineties, and whose treasured possessions nobody seems to want. In an audacious act of journalism driven by personal curiosity and humane tenderness, Clara Beaudoux embarks on *The Madeleine Project*, documenting what she finds on Twitter with text and photographs, introducing the world to an unsung 20th century figure.

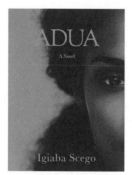

ADUA
BY IGIABA SCEGO

Adua, an immigrant from Somalia to Italy, has lived in Rome for nearly forty years. She came seeking freedom from a strict father and an oppressive regime, but her dreams of film stardom ended in shame. Now that the civil war in Somalia is over, her homeland calls her. She must decide whether to return and reclaim her inheritance, but also how to take charge of her own story and build a future.

IF VENICE DIES
BY SALVATORE SETTIS

Internationally renowned art historian Salvatore Settis ignites a new debate about the Pearl of the Adriatic and cultural patrimony at large. In this fiery blend of history and cultural analysis, Settis argues that "hit-and-run" visitors are turning Venice and other landmark urban settings into shopping malls and theme parks. This is a passionate plea to secure the soul of Venice, written with consummate authority, wide-ranging erudition and élan.

THE MADONNA OF NOTRE DAME
BY ALEXIS RAGOUGNEAU

Fifty thousand people jam into Notre Dame Cathedral to celebrate the Feast of the Assumption. The next morning, a beautiful young woman clothed in white kneels at prayer in a cathedral side chapel. But when someone accidentally bumps against her, her body collapses. She has been murdered. This thrilling novel illuminates shadowy corners of the world's most famous cathedral, shedding light on good and evil with suspense, compassion and wry humor.

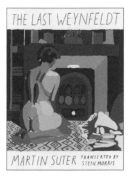

THE LAST WEYNFELDT
BY MARTIN SUTER

Adrian Weynfeldt is an art expert in an international auction house, a bachelor in his mid-fifties living in a grand Zurich apartment filled with costly paintings and antiques. Always correct and well-mannered, he's given up on love until one night—entirely out of character for him—Weynfeldt decides to take home a ravishing but unaccountable young woman and gets embroiled in an art forgery scheme that threatens his buttoned up existence. This refined page-turner moves behind elegant bourgeois facades into darker recesses of the heart.

MOVING THE PALACE
BY CHARIF MAJDALANI

A young Lebanese adventurer explores the wilds of Africa, encountering an eccentric English colonel in Sudan and enlisting in his service. In this lush chronicle of far-flung adventure, the military recruit crosses paths with a compatriot who has dismantled a sumptuous palace and is transporting it across the continent on a camel caravan. This is a captivating modern-day Odyssey in the tradition of Bruce Chatwin and Paul Theroux.

![New Vessel Press logo] New Vessel Press

To purchase these titles and for more information
please visit newvesselpress.com.